A King Production presents…

Stackin' PAPER IX

Buried But Breathing…

A Novel

JOY DEJA KING

Cover concept by Joy Deja King
Cover Model: Joy Deja King

Graphic design: https://anitaart79.wixsite.com/anita
Typesetting: Anita J.

Library of Congress Cataloging-in-Publication Data;
King, Deja Joy
Stackin' Paper Part 9: a novel by Joy Deja King
For complete Library of Congress Copyright info visit;
www.joydejaking.com Twitter: @joydejaking

A King Production
P.O. Box 912, Collierville, TN 38027

A King Production and the above portrayal logo are trademarks of A King Production LLC

This Book is Dedicated To My:

Family, Readers and Supporters.
I LOVE you guys so much. Please believe that!!

-- Joy Deja King

"Grief Carved The Path.
Vengeance Walks It In Blood..."

KING PRODUCTION

Stackin' PAPER

IX

Buried But Breathing

A Novel

JOY DEJA KING

Chapter One

Ashes Don't Lie

The sky over Harlem cracked open like grief itself—gray, swollen, threatening rain. A long line of black Escalades and Benzes stretched down Lenox Avenue, parked like armored guards outside First Corinthian Baptist. Streets were blocked. Security posted on rooftops. The city hadn't seen a funeral this heavy since Biggie. And even then, it didn't hit this close to home.

Amir Taylor's casket gleamed like obsidian, engraved with gold trim and a small, discreet crown etched at the base—a symbol of what he could have been, what he was becoming before the streets swallowed him whole. He was Genesis's son. And the city knew better than to act like that didn't mean something.

Inside, the energy was tight. Supreme sat two rows back, his jaw locked, black gloves on, eyes unmoving. Nico leaned against the far wall, his head bowed, the faintest scar still healing above his brow. Precious sat beside Talisa, both women draped in veils and silence. Angel and Aaliyah were across the aisle, giving nothing but energy—ice-cold and observant.

Genesis stood at the front like a statue carved from war. All black suit. No tie. Black sunglasses. Not a tear, not a tremble. Just presence. His lips hadn't parted since they lowered the empty casket into the ground—a wooden box filled with Amir's childhood trophies, basketball jersey, favorite chain, photos of him as a child, and the last birthday card he'd signed. His silence stretched through the wake, past Talisa's tear-streaked pleas for him to say something, anything. Even when Nico gripped his shoulder and whispered that the family needed to hear his voice to begin healing, Genesis just stared at the grave that held memories instead of his son's body. So, Supreme stepped forward. He looked out at the sea of faces—politicians, killers, pastors, corner kids who once begged Amir for game.

"You all know who he was. You know what he meant to us. What he meant to this city. He ain't just Genesis's son. He was one of us." Supreme paused. Let the silence carry. "But I'm not up here to tell you what you already know. I'm up here to tell the people responsible—we coming. That's it. You took from us. Now we take everything."

Murmurs spread like fire. Genesis didn't move. When the crowd emptied, only a few stayed behind. Talisa brushed her hand against Genesis's back. "Baby, come on. Let's go home."

He shook his head. Stepped closer to the casket. He whispered, "I buried my son. But I ain't buried this war."

That night, a storm rolled in. Lightning split the sky as rain lashed against the penthouse windows overlooking Manhattan, Justina stood barefoot. Her funeral blacks had been shed, replaced by a lace slip that barely covered her thighs. Desmond's fingers traced her spine, his lips brushing against her neck, finding that spot below her ear that always made her surrender. The air crackled between them— familiar heat in a time of grief, desire wrapped in mourning clothes.

"We shouldn't," he whispered against her skin, as his grip tightened. She answered by pulling him down to the leather couch, her kiss tasting of expensive whiskey and unspoken promises.

Down the corridor, Aaliyah pressed her back against the wall, Angel beside her with fury etched across her face.

"Funeral flowers ain't even wilted yet," Angel fumed.

Aaliyah's eyes narrowed to slits. "Amir's body still warm in the ground and she already spreading it wide for her ex."

Desmond's the real snake though. How are you gonna move in on Amir's widow and he's not even cold in his grave. They're already back between the sheets like Amir never existed. Just fuckin' foul."

They stood in silence, the weight of the day's burial heavy on their shoulders. Both women knew that karma worked in cycles—and Justina's day of reckoning was coming, one way or another.

Six Months Later...

Genesis sat in his office, the city sprawled out before him like a chessboard of shadows and light. The chair creaked under his weight as he stared out at New York. Streetlights flickered on across the boroughs—Harlem to Brooklyn, Queens to the Bronx—each one a soldier in his silent army. Six months since the funeral, and the city still bent to his will, every block and corner rebuilt by his hand after they'd tried to burn his empire to the ground while he was in mourning over the death of his only son. Dressed in a tailored charcoal suit that whispered of power and precision, he exuded a quiet authority that belied the storm brewing within him.

Precious sat across from him, embodying her usual air of poise and control, as she relayed the details of what had recently transpired during her trip to Houston. She gave an in-depth blow by blow of how Cortez, Maverick's right-hand-man—had nearly put Genevieve in the ground, holding her thumb and index finger an inch apart to show just how close the hit had come.

"My baby sister." Genesis' voice dropped to a dangerous whisper. Blood rushed to his temples as Precious laid out how Cortez had Genevieve in his sights—crosshairs a breath away from his sister's head. Each detail Precious offered made his jaw clench tighter, the muscle in his cheek jumping like a live wire. He rolled his shoulders back, trying to ease the familiar weight settling between them—the one that came with knowing everyone he loved lived or died by his next move.

Genesis's phone vibrated, cutting through the heavy silence with the urgency of a gunshot. A message from Caleb flashed on the screen, detailing suspicious activity near one of their warehouses. The walls of his office seemed to close in. A familiar ache settled in his chest, a constant reminder of the gaping hole left by his son, Amir. His gaze drifted to the photo on his desk, Talisa's smile frozen in time beside the bright eyes of their son.

Fingers lingering on the frame, Genesis shifted his thought process making a swift decision, his voice carving through the tension as he told Precious to bring Supreme and Nico in for an emergency meeting. They needed to strategize.

Precious glanced down at his phone. "What did the text message say?" she questioned.

"I rather discuss it when everyone is here," Genesis said, seeming lost in his thoughts.

Precious rose from her seat, the rustle of her clothes crisp in the otherwise silent room. She knew it was best not to ask too many questions when Genesis' voice took on that edge—like a blade honed by grief and desperation. As she moved towards the door, she felt his gaze on her back, heavy as a hand. She paused at the threshold, turning to meet his eyes. They were dark, almost black, reflecting the city lights like shards of broken glass.

The office door clicked shut behind her, leaving Genesis alone with his thoughts. The room felt too quiet. His mind flicked back to the funeral. The rain, the cold, the hollow echo of Supreme's words in the church. "We coming." It was more than a promise; it was a declaration of war. A war that seemed everlasting, a war that Maverick McClay seemed eager to continue. Genesis opened his eyes, his reflection staring back at him from the glass. The city lights blinked through the floor-to-ceiling windows, casting eerie shadows that danced like ghosts on his eyelids. Amir's ghost. Always there, always waiting.

Genesis once again stared at the photo of
Talisa and Amir, their smiles a painful reminder
of what he had lost. The glass surface was cool
under his fingertips, a stark contrast to the heat
rising in his chest. He remembered Amir's laughter, the way it filled a room, and the pride in his
eyes when he talked about the future. All of it
gone, snuffed out like a candle in the wind.

Precious' heels clicked against the polished
floor as she walked down the hall dialing Supreme first. He answered on the second ring.

"Hey baby, what's up," Supreme's voice
sounded gruff like he'd been sleep.

Precious lowered her voice. "Genesis needs
you and Nico at the office. Now. Something came
through on his phone that's got him wound tighter than I've seen in weeks. I'm concerned."

"Okay. I'll call Nico. We'll be there."

"Thanks babe. Love you."

"Love you too," Supreme said hanging up
the phone. The room still dark around him. He
swung his legs out of bed, his mind already racing ahead to what could have Genesis so on edge.
He dressed quickly, preparing for the chaos of
the night in a city that never slept. Not when
there were always threats, whispers hinting at
the next storm. He checked his gun, the weight

of it familiar and reassuring in his hand. Whatever was happening, he'd be ready. They'd face it head-on, like they always did.

Chapter Two

Smoke Signals

The city shimmered like a mirage from the 43rd floor of Genesis's office. Below, traffic snarled and pulsed, indifferent to the war brewing be hind closed doors. He sat still as stone, elbows on the glass desk, eyes cutting through the skyline like a sniper's scope. His empire hadn't just survived—it had evolved. New front businesses, new routes, new partnerships. But none of that erased the phantom weight of Amir. A knock broke the silence.

Precious entered without waiting for a response, her black trench cinched at the waist, and her presence crisp as a blade. "Supreme and Nico are on their way," she said, sliding a folder onto the desk. "Things got sidetracked after you received that text. So, I didn't have a chance to give you one last update about what has been transpiring in Houston. Word is, one of Maverick's new guys is moving aggressive. The one who took over after Cortez got clipped. Ruthless. Tactical. No loose ends."

Genesis didn't look at the folder. "This nigga just won't stop," he grumbled.

"Maverick will stop once we kill him. And we will kill him," Precious stated with certainty.

"Blood gon' answer for blood, no doubt," he replied.

The door opened again. Supreme walked in first, dressed in all black and Nico followed, dressed impeccable in a tailored suit, his eyes colder than usual.

"I left Kyra at a very expensive restaurant, and I ain't even touch my food," Nico complained, "so this better be important."

Genesis gave a dry chuckle. "Trust me, it is. But I do apologize for interrupting your dinner date."

He stood, walked around the desk, and

tossed Caleb's message on the table. "Warehouse on 117th got tailed two nights in a row. Same grey Charger circling the block. Same plates. Same time."

Nico leaned in. "Cameras?"

"Disabled," Precious answered. "Which tells me whoever did it has inside intel."

Supreme folded his arms. "That Charger move like a ghost. That's too clean to be street-level."

"I already sent a runner to Philly," Genesis said. "Caleb's watching the ports. But this ain't just about tracking cars anymore. I think Maverick's positioning for another hit."

Nico scoffed. "That nigga never stopped positioning."

Genesis turned to Supreme. "You still got the roster on that gun crew from Trenton?"

"Most of 'em. Why?"

"Put the word out. I want eyes in Jersey, Queens Uptown. If this is about to turn hot, I want the heat coming from us first."

Nico raised an eyebrow. "You looking to spark something?"

"I'm looking to end something before it grows teeth," Genesis said. The room went quiet.

Supreme broke the silence with a loaded question. "What about Shiffon?"

Genesis's expression didn't change. "What about her?"

"Did Caleb handle that?" Supreme pressed.

Nico eyed Genesis. "That was a cold-blooded demonstration to have that young man take Shiffon out. If he was able to follow through on that, he ready to run his own shit."

"You're right, especially since Shiffon was pregnant. You know I was against having her killed but I understand. Maverick took your child, you wanted to take his too," Precious added, unease etched into her face.

Genesis didn't flinch. "You know what matters? That I don't bury another child. That I don't lose my sister, my wife, or one of you. That I don't watch this whole city spin out while I sit quiet in a tower." He paused. "They drew first blood. And my patience has run out."

Nico stepped forward, ready to move past the ominous vibe in the room. "So, what's the play, boss?"

Genesis stared out the window, looking down at the city that once raised and nearly broke him. "Same as always," he said. "We stay low until we can strike high. I want Maverick blind. And

I want every muthafucker playing both sides caught in the crossfire."

Just then, Genesis's phone buzzed again. A single message.

***We need to talk. Tonight. Alone.* —Caleb**

He stared at the screen. Caleb didn't spook easy. For him to request a private meeting meant something was bubbling in Philly—and it wasn't good. Genesis slid the phone into his pocket. "I'm heading out tonight."

"Where to?" Supreme asked.

"Philly."

"Alone?" Precious shot him a look.

"I'll take two drivers, no detail."

He looked around the room—Nico, Supreme, Precious. His inner circle. His only circle.

"Y'all handle things here. I'll be back before sunrise."

Supreme nodded. "You got it."

As Genesis grabbed his coat, he turned once more to the skyline.

"Start watching everyone," he said. "That includes our own." Then he left the room, silence trailing behind him like smoke.

The warehouse Caleb used for meetings wasn't in West Philly, or South. It was hidden deep in a no-name industrial pocket near the shipyards— graffiti-scarred, windowless, quiet. The kind of place where things happened, and no one asked questions. Genesis arrived just after midnight in a blacked-out Escalade, two drivers posted up outside with eyes sharp and triggers looser than usual.

Caleb waited inside, leaning against a steel support beam, hoodie half-zipped, Jordans still dusty from the block. He didn't stand up straight when Genesis entered—didn't need to. He wasn't a soldier anymore. He was family.

"You came alone?" Caleb asked, voice low.

"I don't do alone," Genesis replied. "But my people know when to stay outside."

They dapped, firm but respectful. Genesis scanned the room. No chairs. No table. Just concrete, silence, and tension.

"What's this about?" Genesis asked.

Caleb handed over a burner phone. "That's a screenshot of a message intercepted by one of my people up in Camden. Look at the sender ID."

Genesis narrowed his eyes. The number was local—but the name attached to it hit like a gut punch.

'M. McClay – Level 2 Clearance.'

"What the fuck is this?" Genesis asked.

Caleb stepped back; arms crossed. "Somebody in your circle—maybe mine—is feeding him intel. Warehouse routes. Driver schedules. Even the names of low-level runners who just got patched in last month. That's not street gossip. That's internal."

Genesis's jaw flexed. "You trust the source?"

"I vetted it six ways before I brought it to you."

The silence stretched. Genesis turned the phone off, slipping it into his pocket. He walked a slow circle around the room, then stopped. "What else?"

Caleb hesitated. "There's whispers about a move down south. Maverick ain't just aiming at you now. He's circling Houston again. One of his lieutenants is sending bodies to test Genevieve's defenses."

"Already handled," Genesis said coldly.

Another beat passed. Then Genesis turned and fixed his eyes on Caleb. "And what about Shiffon?"

Caleb blinked. "What about her?"

"I gave you a direct order," Genesis said, voice sharp. "She was carrying that muthafuckas seed. I asked you once before and you said it was done. Now I'm asking again. Because if she's alive and Maverick finds her—"

"She's gone." Caleb said it without baulking. "I handled it."

"You sure?"

Caleb nodded; eyes steady. "Positive."

Genesis stared at him a long moment. Then he nodded once. "Alright."

But something in the air shifted—barely there, a tremor beneath the surface. Caleb didn't break eye contact, but he didn't move either. Genesis held the silence for a beat too long, then finally said: "Good. That chapter needed to be closed."

Caleb didn't speak. Didn't need to.

Genesis checked his watch. "I'm heading back before dawn. Keep the intel flowing. And if this mole's close... I want a name. I want proof."

"You'll have it," Caleb promised.

Genesis paused at the door. "And Caleb?"

"Yeah?"

"If you lied to me... I'll know," Genesis warned, stepping into the night, the door shutting behind him.

Caleb listened as the echo of the door closing faded into the vast emptiness of the warehouse.

The air felt thicker, the silence louder. He took a deep breath, the dust and decay of the warehouse filling his nostrils. The place was a grim reminder of the world they operated in—dark, dirty, and dangerous words hung heavy, a weight he couldn't shake off so easily. "If you lied to me... I'll know." It wasn't a threat; it was a fact, cold and hard as the concrete beneath his feet. The promise of consequences real.

He pushed off the steel beam, the chill of the metal lingering on his back as he began to pace. The room felt smaller, the shadows darker. His mind raced, flicking through memories and calculations like a deck of cards. Shiffon's face flashed in his thoughts, her eyes wide with fear and defiance. He shook his head, dispelling the image. He'd done what he had to. There was no room for self-doubt, not now, not ever.

Chapter Three

The Mercer Effect

The warehouse smelled like rust, gasoline, and terror.

In the center of the room, duct-taped to a steel chair, was a man known on the streets as Buckie. Mid-level supplier. Loyal until he wasn't. Blood leaked from his nose and mouth, pooling at his boots. Across from him stood the reason his heartbeat sounded like war drums inside his own chest—Riot Mercer.

Young, wild, and dangerous in that unpredictable way, Riot didn't wear suits like his deceased brother Cortez. He wore a black Carhartt jacket over a wifebeater, black cargos and Timberlands caked with street residue. His gold fronts glinted every time he smiled—and Riot smiled a lot. Especially when people bled.

"Y'know what pisses me off the most, Buckie?" Riot asked, crouching down to eye level. "A coward that acts like a gangster 'til it's time to stand on business."

Buckie whimpered; lips too swollen to speak. Riot reached into his pocket, pulled out a chrome straight razor, and flicked it open like a habit.

"You was eatin' good. Ridin' off my brother's name. Now Cortez dead and you out here makin' side deals? With Genesis' people?" Riot shook his head slowly. "That's like pissin' on the grave and askin' for flowers."

A man in a ski mask stepped forward, holding a phone. "He's been texting someone on the low. Trying to flip."

Riot took the phone, scrolled, and saw it— unsent message draft to an unknown number: *I'm ready to talk. I can give you Riot's drops.*

He stood, turned to the others. "Run the camera."

One of the men set up a phone on a tripod,

framing Buckie in the shot. Riot stepped in front of him, razor still in hand.

"This is what happens when you cross family," Riot said to the lens. "To anyone out there thinkin' about snitchin', flippin', or even dreamin' about movin' against us—don't."

He turned, wiped the razor clean across Buckie's hoodie, then stepped back and nodded once. A single gunshot ended it. The sound echoed through the empty warehouse. One of the masked men walked over and spray-painted a crown with an X over it on the wall behind Buckie's lifeless body.

Riot looked into the camera one last time. "Y'all mournin' Cortez. I'm makin' examples."

He shut off the camera and tossed the blood-streaked phone on the body. Then he turned to his team. "Burn it."

As they doused the chair and body in accelerant, Riot walked out into the alley, lit a Newport with steady hands, and stared at the skyline. Cortez's old territory was slipping, and Genesis's people were getting too bold. That was about to change.

Maverick McClay sat in the private screening room at his waterfront compound in Miami. The room was dark except for the glow of the projector screen. He sat alone in a high-back leather chair, a crystal tumbler of Rémy XO in one hand, cigar untouched in the other. The video Riot sent played again in front of him—no sound, just the raw visual of violence unfolding under streetlights.

Riot didn't flinch in the footage. Didn't yell. Didn't celebrate. He moved like a shark through water—calm, efficient, and inevitable.

The camera caught it all: the terrified man pleading, the precision of Riot's blade, the cold stare as blood splattered across the pavement. One of his soldiers tried to look away. Riot grabbed his jaw and forced him to watch.

Maverick leaned forward, elbows on knees, watching the moment Riot whispered something to the victim before delivering the final blow. He rewound that frame, zoomed in.

"You picked the wrong side," Riot had said. The words weren't loud, but they landed like thunder.

Maverick exhaled smoke through his nose and finally cracked a grin.

"Little Cortez," he muttered to himself. "Only

louder... and a hell of a lot messier."

He reached for his phone, dialed without looking at the screen.

"Vernon," he said when the line picked up. "It's time we let the city know Riot Mercer is active. Put the word out—he's taking over his brothers connects, his corners, and anyone who got a problem with it can meet their maker early."

He hung up. Took a sip. Then hit play again.

Not because he needed to watch it. But because he liked to. Maverick took another drag of his cigar, the smoke curling around his lips as he watched the flames dance on the screen. The video ended, but the image of Riot's cold stare lingered in his mind. That kid had something—a ruthlessness that couldn't be taught. It was a shame Cortez wasn't alive to see it. But then again, Cortez never would've approved of that raw savagery—instead worried his little brother was becoming something even the streets would fear. Riot had that look, the one that said he wasn't afraid to die, wasn't afraid to kill. It reminded him of... himself.

Maverick took another sip of his Rémy, the liquid burning a path down his throat, a pleasant contrast to the cold air of the screening room. The ice clinked against the glass as he set it down, his eyes still fixed on the now-black screen. Riot was a variable he hadn't fully considered until now. The kid was brutal, unpredictable—a wildcard that could tip the scales in this never-ending war with Genesis.

He stood, the leather chair creaking under his weight, and walked to the floor-to-ceiling windows. Outside, the Miami lights sparkled off the water, a stark contrast to the dark alleys and grimy streets of New York. He missed the grit, the constant hum of tension. Miami was too clean, too bright. It didn't have the same pulse, the same hunger. Miami wasn't about pleasure—it was strictly business. The plan was in motion, but Maverick wouldn't move without perfect intel. The phone in his pocket vibrated against his thigh, interrupting his calculation. He was hoping this was Vernon calling back with confirmation, then the pieces would finally align.

Maverick pulled the phone from his pocket. The caller ID flashed Vernon's name, and he swiped to answer, pressing it to his ear as he turned away from the windows. The city lights reflected off the glass, casting a fractured glow across his face. "Talk to me," Maverick said, his voice a low rumble. He took another drag of his cigar, the smoke curling around him like a shroud.

Vernon's voice came through, steady and serious. "Justina's back in Miami. And she's not alone. Desmond Blackwell—the ex-husband—he's been at her place almost daily. Sometimes stays hours. Twice now, he hasn't left till morning."

Maverick's lips curled into a cold smile around his cigar. He took a slow drag, the ember glowing bright. "Seems the grieving widow's bed is still warm, and they say Amir's body isn't even cold yet." His expression hardened into something between amusement and contempt. "How... convenient. Continue to keep tabs on Justina, and Riot. I'll be in touch," he said ending the call.

Maverick took another long drag, letting the smoke fill his lungs before exhaling slowly. The news of Justina and Desmond was more than just a distraction, it was a potential chink in Genesis's armor. He walked back to his desk, and stubbed out his cigar in the crystal ashtray, the embers dying with a hiss. He leaned back in his chair, considering the implications. Her indiscretions could be a weakness to exploit, a way to drive a wedge deeper into Genesis's inner circle. But he needed more—more intel, more leverage. His mind was already racing, analyzing the next moves. If Justina was vulnerable, she could be manipulated.

Chapter Four

Trigger Points

Genesis stood at the head of the long, obsidian conference table like a war general in a glass bunker. The New York skyline behind him was all cold steel and fire-stained sky. The massive windows reflected the people seated before him like ghosts of the empire he built.

Supreme leaned back in his chair, arms folded tight across his chest. Nico sat with his phone face-down, jaw tense, eyes scanning the room. Precious, chic as always, wore all black with her hair pinned in a high bun—sharp as her mind.

She had always been a reliable friend to Genesis, but now he not only relied on her in his personal life but also in his business. And Caleb—Genesis' young protégé from Philly—sat off to the side, hoodie pulled low, tension leaking out of his posture like steam.

"Let's be clear," Genesis began, voice low but final. "We ain't in defense mode anymore. We ain't reacting. We're moving." He tossed a burner phone onto the table. "That came from Caleb. Text this morning. Warehouse hit last night in the Bronx. Light work, but it's the message that matters."

Nico sat forward. "Who we thinking?"

"Riot Mercer."

The room shifted. Even Supreme raised an eyebrow.

"Little brother of Cortez," Precious muttered. "Didn't know he was still breathing."

"He's not just breathing," Genesis said. "He's trying to fill Cortez's shoes with rocket fuel and razor wire. The kid wants to be Maverick's right hand."

Caleb stiffened. "We ain't seen him in Philly."

"You will," Genesis replied. "And if you do, don't make a move till I say so." He looked directly at Caleb now and as if to catch him off guard he asked, "Speaking of moves... That Shiffon situation I told you to handle. It's done, right?"

Caleb's throat bobbed. "Yeah. It's done."

Genesis stared at him a moment longer. "No loose ends?"

"None," Caleb said, steady.

Precious studied the exchange, her gaze shifting between them like a pendulum. Part of her prayed Caleb had spared Shiffon and the baby—not that she'd admit it aloud. Genesis needed loyalty right now, not mercy. Something flickered across Caleb's face when he answered. A hesitation. Barely perceptible, but she caught it. A micro expression flashed across his face, there and gone. She filed the observation away, keeping her manicured nails pressed against her thigh. This wasn't the moment. Not with war brewing and Genesis already seeing ghosts everywhere he looked.

Genesis broke the silence. "Good. Then we focus on the leak. Somebody feeding info to Maverick's camp. They knew about the Brooklyn safehouse. The Jersey port run. Even whispers about Nico's crew in Harlem."

Nico blinked. "You saying somebody in our camp is runnin' they fuckin' mouth to our enemy?"

"I'm saying we don't assume loyalty any-more. Not from anyone."

The room went quiet.

Genesis turned to Supreme. "Thank you for keeping an eye on everything in Jersey and Up-town. I know you been watching, has anyone been moving different?"

"Nope, but I'll stay on top of it."

Genesis then turned to Nico. "How are things going with the nurse?"

Nico hesitated. "Shit is good with Kyra. What that gotta do with this?"

"It don't. Not directly. But stay sharp. Love is a distraction, and right now distractions can get you killed."

Nico nodded; jaw still tight.

"Caleb, you heading back to Philly tonight. I want eyes on all incoming product and anyone asking the wrong questions. You report to me di-rectly."

"Bet," Caleb said, standing.

Genesis looked around the room. "This ain't just about turf anymore. It's about blood. They came for mine. Now we come for theirs. But we do it smart. No more reactions. We strike where it hurts."

Everyone stood.

Supreme nodded. "We ready."

Precious grabbed her phone. "I'll call the shooters we can trust."

As they filed out, Genesis stayed behind, eyes on the skyline. His son was dead. His empire was under siege. But he was still standing. Trigger points were everywhere. And a new war had only just begun. He turned from the window, the city lights gleaming like a battlefield behind him. He could feel the ghost of Amir in the room, the weight of his son's absence a physical pressure on his chest. He rubbed his sternum as if that could ease the ache, but it was a pain that wouldn't be soothed. Not until Maverick and everyone involved paid in blood.

He walked back to the table, picking up the burner phone Caleb had brought him. He scrolled through the messages again, committing every detail to memory. Riot Mercer was a new player, a wildcard, and Genesis didn't like surprises.

His fingers tightened around the phone, the plastic creaking under his grip. He slipped it into his pocket, and paced back to the window, the city sprawled out like a circuit board, lights blinking in patterns only he could decipher. His reflection stared back at him, the lines around his eyes etched deeper by the harsh glow. He looked tired, worn down by the constant battle. War had a way of aging a man, turning his soul old before its time. But behind the exhaustion, his gaze was still lethal—that unmistakable warning that made soldiers and rivals alike step back. The same hunger that refused to let the streets swallow him whole. Genesis hadn't survived bullets, betrayal and not even being able to bury his own son properly just to fold now. His empire wasn't built on surrender, and neither was his soul.

Genesis's thoughts turned to Riot Mercer, the name alone a spark ready to ignite a powder keg. The kid was hungry, reckless—a dangerous combination. But there was something else, a niggling sensation in his gut that told him Riot wasn't just a loose cannon; he was a pawn. And Maverick was the puppet master, pulling strings from behind the scenes.

Miami's heat didn't just sit on the skin—it burrowed into the bones. Maverick stood barefoot on the marble terrace of his Biscayne Bay mansion, shirt unbuttoned, diamond chain glinting in the sunrise. A glass of fresh-pressed juice sweated in his hand, but he wasn't drinking it. His focus was across the water, watching the yacht drift by like it didn't have a care in the world. That was the thing about luxury—it lulled people into thinking they were safe.

But Maverick? He never felt safe. He didn't believe in peace. Only strategy.

Behind him, Vernon stepped out. "I got the report on Justina."

Maverick turned; eyes sharp. "Talk to me."

"She hasn't been living in the house she shared with Amir. She's staying at a condo in Brickell. And like I previously mentioned, back in the sheets with her ex-husband."

"Desmond," Maverick said with a sneer, like the name tasted foul. "The weak link with good suits and soft hands."

Vernon nodded. "They don't even hide it. Paparazzi caught them holding hands at the Wynwood Art Walk. Looked domestic as hell."

Maverick's jaw ticked. "You said she still checkin' in with Genesis?"

"Not directly," Vernon replied. "But she talks to Talisa. Sends photos of the baby. Keeping the peace."

Maverick turned his back to the view. "Peace is a lie. People like Justina don't stay quiet unless they scared... or distracted."

He walked back inside, the soles of his feet silent against the imported stone floors. The mansion reeked of money—floor-to-ceiling glass, custom leather, abstract art worth more than most people's houses. But the opulence didn't soften him. It was camouflage.

He picked up the manila envelope off the kitchen counter, opened it. Photos of Justina. At the park with her son. Pulling into valet at a brunch spot. At home on her balcony in a robe, talking on the phone, her face worried but still beautiful.

"Her man's a fool," Maverick muttered. "Can't keep a woman like that safe." He looked up at Vernon. "You said the kid's what... three now?"

"Almost four."

"Still playing the loyal widow for Amir's parents, but got her ex-husband back in her bed," Maverick smiled, dark and cruel. "That tells me something. She ain't healed. She's still bleeding. And anybody still bleeding can be touched."

Vernon nodded slowly, already knowing where this was headed. "So, what's the move?"

"I want someone close to her. Not no loud-mouth or street cat. Somebody clean. Professional. Who can sit across from her in a yoga class and make her feel seen. Who can tell her she deserves more. A new start. Someone who don't look like a setup—until it's too late."

Vernon scratched his jaw. "You want her seduced?"

"I want her exposed," Maverick corrected. "Her fears, her regrets, her needs. If I can get her to turn... even a little bit? Genesis will break. That's his grandson's mother. Amir's widow. If I touch her, I touch his legacy. His bloodline. And he'll bleed for real."

Vernon whistled low. "That's a tight move."

Maverick walked toward the hidden panel in the wall and pulled it open. Inside was a digital screen with rotating dossiers—names, faces, assets. He tapped through until he landed on a profile: *Marcus Blaine. 32. Former model. Background in wellness coaching. Low profile. No priors. Attractive. Manipulative. Loyal to the dollar.*

"This one," Maverick said. "Get him briefed. First contact within the week. I want him on her like perfume."

Vernon smirked. "You sure he got the discipline for something like this?"

Maverick leaned in close, voice like venom. "If he doesn't, he'll find out what it means to disappoint me. And so will she."

Chapter Five

Collateral Moves

On the outskirts of Philadelphia there was a small house—one story, peeling white paint, ivy strangling the sides like the past trying to take hold. A rusted wind chime clinked against the night breeze. Inside, the glow of a muted television flickered across the living room. Some old 90s sitcom rerun played to no one in particular.

Mia sat on the couch, blanket draped over her legs, a half-eaten bowl of popcorn resting on the coffee table. Her eyes were fixed on the screen, but her mind was miles away. She didn't flinch when the door creaked open behind her. She knew the rhythm of those footsteps.

Caleb entered, his hoodie damp from the mist outside, eyes scanning the room like he expected opps to jump.

"You're late," Mia said quietly, not looking at him.

Caleb locked the door behind him, slid off his jacket. "Had to circle the block twice. Thought I saw a car with Jersey tags." He walked over, bent down to kiss her cheek. She didn't lean in.

"It's getting riskier," she murmured, eyes still on the screen.

"I know."

Caleb straightened and moved toward the hallway. Mia stood, followed.

"Did you bring the vitamins?" she asked.

He nodded, pulling a small paper bag from his backpack. "Prenatals. The good kind. Organic."

They walked together down the narrow hallway, every board creaking under their steps. At the end of the hall, Caleb paused at a door. He knocked once, softly, then pushed it open.

The bedroom smelled like lavender and baby powder. The lights were low. In the bed,

Shiffon lay curled on her side, a mountain of pillows tucked between her knees and under her arm. Her belly was round, taut, rising and falling with slow, measured breaths. She didn't wake.

Mia leaned against the doorframe; arms crossed. "You sure this is still the move?"

Caleb stared at Shiffon, the corners of his mouth tight. "It has to be."

"She's almost full term," Mia said, voice low. "And Genesis thinks she's dead. You lied to him to protect her, Caleb."

He turned to Mia, eyes hard. "I know what I did."

"And if he finds out—"

"He won't," Caleb snapped, sharper than he meant to. Then softer: "I'm not trying to protect Shiffon for *me*. I'm doing this for the baby."

Mia's voice cracked. "And when the baby's here? Then what?"

Caleb exhaled slowly. "Then I figure it out."

Silence hung between them, heavy as grief. Shiffon shifted in her sleep, her hand sliding over her stomach protectively. Caleb stepped inside, setting the vitamins on the nightstand beside a glass of water. He brushed a hand gently across her forehead, smoothing away a stray curl.

"She doesn't even know what's waiting on

the other side of that door," Mia said, almost to herself.

"I'm trying to keep her in a world where it doesn't matter," Caleb replied. "At least until she gives birth. After that..." He didn't finish.

Mia looked at him like she wanted to scream, or cry, or both. Instead, she walked away.

Caleb stayed in the room a moment longer, staring down at Shiffon. "Just a little longer," he whispered.

But the lie was already too big. And the clock was ticking.

Justina pulled her curls into a loose bun as she stepped into the tranquil, citrus-scented air of the wellness center tucked between high-rises in downtown Miami. The chaos of her life— Desmond's confusing affection, the whispers behind her back, the ghost of Amir—faded just a little when she was here. No one asked questions. No one called her "Amir Taylor's widow." In this room, she was just Justina. A woman trying to breathe.

She signed in and smiled at the reception-ist, who nodded toward Studio B. Her hips still ached from chasing little Desi around the condo all morning. Yoga was her peace now.

Inside, the studio was dimly lit, all neutral tones and soft instrumental music humming low through ceiling speakers. Only a few other clients were present, stretching in silence.

That's when she saw him. Tall. Athletic. Skin like brushed copper and eyes that didn't linger too long, but just long enough to register presence. He wore a black tank, joggers, and a calm expression that didn't match the Miami ego she'd grown used to. Something about him felt... professional but grounded. Like he had nothing to prove.

He nodded once. Respectful. Distant.

She nodded back, a flicker of curiosity crossing her face. She took her usual spot on the second mat from the front.

The instructor entered moments later, a petite Brazilian woman with a voice that could put a hurricane to sleep. "Let's begin."

As the class moved through sun salutations and deep stretches, Justina caught glimpses of him. His form was precise, like he'd done this for years. No awkwardness. Confident. Just breath and movement. She caught herself watching longer than she should've.

After class, she grabbed her water bottle and headed for the exit, her mind already drifting to Desmond and whether or not Dominique would call again. She was halfway to the parking garage when she heard the voice behind her.

"Excuse me. You left your mat."

She turned, startled, and saw him—mat in hand, a hint of a smile at the corner of his mouth.

"Oh," she said, a little breathless. "Thank you."

"No problem," he said. "I'm Marcus, by the way. First time seeing you here."

She smiled faintly. "Justina. I come pretty often, actually. I guess our schedules never lined up."

He handed her the mat. "Well, I'll be around. You have great control. Your breathing's solid."

She tilted her head, amused. "You sound like a coach."

He chuckled. "Old habit. I used to do wellness consulting back in L.A. Body mechanics, recovery, all that."

Justina looked down at the mat, then back at him. "Well, I appreciate the compliment. See you around?"

"Definitely," Marcus said, voice smooth as silk.

He waited until she turned the corner before pulling his phone from his waistband. A quick text, simple and clean:

Initial contact made. She's receptive. Not suspicious. Yet.

Justina walked away, feeling a strange mix of curiosity and discomfort. Marcus seemed genuine, but there was something about him that didn't quite fit the usual mold of guys she met. There was a stark contrast to the hungry eyes she usually encountered in Miami, the kind that undressed you before you even said hello. She shook her head slightly, attributing it to her own paranoia. Ever since Amir's death, she'd been on edge, always looking over her shoulder, always suspicious.

She reached her black Range Rover and as she opened the door, Justina paused, her eyes scanning the dimly lit parking area. A shiver ran down her spine, a familiar sense of unease settling in her stomach. She couldn't shake the feeling of being watched, a constant companion since she'd moved back to Miami.

Sliding into the driver's seat, she locked the doors immediately, her breath coming a little faster. She started the engine, the purr of the car filling did little to drown out the noise in her head. Justina gripped the steering wheel, her palms slick with a thin layer of sweat. She checked the mirrors, her eyes darting from one to the other, scanning for any sign of a tail. The parking garage was stark and cold, concrete pillars casting long, eerie shadows that seemed to twist and writhe in the corners of her vision. She reversed sharply, the tires squealing against the smooth floor, and pulled out of the space.

Her heart pounded in her chest as she navigated the winding exit ramp, the fluorescent lights flickering overhead like a bad omen. She could feel the weight of unseen eyes on her, the sensation prickling her skin like a thousand tiny needles. It was always like this—the paranoia, the constant feeling of being watched. She had tried to dismiss it, as it was exhausting, but she couldn't afford to let her guard down. Not now, not ever.

As she turned onto Biscayne Boulevard, her phone buzzed in the cup holder, the screen lighting up with Desmond's name. Justina glanced at the phone, his name flashing like a warning sign, a beacon of complication. She hesitated, her thumb hovering over the answer button. The traffic light turned red, and she hit the brakes a little too hard, the car jerking to a stop. She picked up the phone, swiped to answer, and put it on speaker, setting it back in the cup holder as if it might burn her.

"Hey," Desmond's voice filled the car, smooth and warm, a contrast to the cold knot in her stomach.

"Hey," she replied, her eyes scanning the rearview mirror again. The car behind her was a nondescript sedan, the driver a blurry silhouette. She couldn't shake the feeling of being followed, but she forced her attention back to the conversation.

"You, okay? You sound tense," Desmond's voice was a low rumble through the speaker, a familiar sound that used to bring comfort. Now, it just added to the noise in her head. Justina forced her eyes back to the road, the lights of Miami blurring into a neon streak as she accelerated through the intersection.

"I'm fine," she lied, her grip tightening on the wheel, keeping a watchful eye on the car behind her, which kept a steady distance, too steady. She switched lanes, her heart thudding in her chest as the headlights followed. Coincidence? Or something more sinister? She couldn't take any chances. Not after everything that had happened. She took the next exit, her tires humming against the asphalt as she veered onto a quiet side street. The headlights remained, a menacing presence in her mirror. Her breath hitched, but she refused to panic. She'd been through worse, survived more. She reached into her purse. Justina's hand trembled slightly as she felt the cold metal of the small gun she kept tucked away in her purse. A precaution she hated but couldn't live without.

There had been a long pause on the other end, a silence that felt heavier than it should have. "You sure?" Desmond pressed. His voice cut through her haze. "You sound like you're driving a getaway car, not heading home from yoga."

The sedan's high beams vanished at the intersection, leaving only darkness in her rearview. Justina exhaled slowly, questioning whether danger had been real or just another ghost conjured by her paranoia.

"Justina? You still there?" Desmond's voice cut through her thoughts like a knife. His voice was full of concern.

She swallowed hard, steadied her breathing. "Yeah, sorry," she managed, forcing her voice to stay level while her pulse hammered against her throat. "These night classes are killing me. By the time I'm done with all those poses, I'm exhausted and can barely keep my eyes open for the drive home."

Desmond's voice dropped lower, that protective edge she both craved and resented creeping in. "Then babe, maybe find a morning class instead. These streets ain't safe for you to be out alone after dark."

Justina's fingers brushed against the cold metal in her purse. "I can handle myself. I keep the piece you gave me close at all times."

She turned sharply onto her street, the Range Rover's tires hugging the asphalt. Her condo building rose up ahead, a gleaming tower of glass and steel. She pulled into the underground parking garage, the automatic gate closing behind her with a finality that did little to ease her nerves. She parked in her designated spot, engine idling as she scanned the garage. Empty, except for a few familiar cars belonging to neighbors.

Desmond's voice softened. "You fought me on carrying at first, but I'm glad you decided to listen. After everything that's happened, you can't be too careful in this city."

Justina nodded to herself as she slid out of the Range. "I hear you," she said, her fingers grazing the outline of the gun through her designer purse. The cold metal beneath the fabric sent a chill through her that was equal parts fear and reassurance. Her senses remained heightened. The air was cool against her skin, carrying a faint scent of exhaust and the distant crash of waves against the shore. She glanced around, then a figure emerged from the shadows—a security guard making his rounds. She released a breath she hadn't realized she was holding. Even in the safety of her building, her nerves remained raw, her senses tuned to threats that might not exist. The security guard nodded as he passed, and Justina returned the gesture with practiced calm. She'd learned the hard way that in her world, yesterday's allies could become tomorrow's enemies. Her hand remained on her purse, fingers inches from the gun—a woman who'd rather pull the trigger first than end up in the ground.

Chapter Six

War Room

The conference room was built for luxury— sleek marble table, leather chairs, skyline view stretching past the Hudson—but tonight, it felt more like a bunker. Genesis sat at the head of the table, flanked by Supreme and Nico. Precious was next to him, tablet in hand, with Caleb sitting directly across from her. The only light came from the screen on the far wall—maps, surveillance footage, and movement charts blinking in red.

"First off," Genesis said, voice lethal, "we can't fuck this up. Too much on the line." Everyone went quiet. "Cortez is gone, but that opened the door for someone hungrier, his demonic little brother, Riot Mercer." The name hung in the room like smoke. "The nigga young, wild and trigger-happy. He wants blood to make his name—and he wants *mine*."

Caleb tapped a button on the screen. A face popped up—grimy mugshot-style image. Braids, a gold grill, hollowed-out eyes. "Riot's already making noise," Caleb explained. "Took out one of Cortez's former lieutenants on camera. We got it from one of our Miami sources. Maverick's crew leaked it like a mixtape."

"Trying to send a message," Supreme muttered, his fingers flexing.

Genesis nodded. "Which means it's time to respond." He stood, walked slowly toward the window, and looked out at the night. "We're tightening every loop—logistics, transportation, club fronts, and security around everyone tied to me. From Talisa and Genie down to Justina and my grandson."

Nico leaned forward. "You want a preemptive strike?"

Genesis turned from the window. "I want to hit them where it does the most damage. But not reckless. Not yet. That's what Riot wants. He's emotional. We're strategic. He's putting bodies on corners. We freeze his pipeline instead. No product, no paydays. Let his men start asking questions."

Caleb nodded. "We already started hitting stash houses in Newark and Trenton. Quiet but effective. Dried up one spot in Houston last week. Made it look like an inside job."

"Good," Genesis said. "I'ma give Renny a heads up what we're doing. We need to keep him in the loop since Houston's his city. I want whispers in Maverick's camp, wondering if his new golden boy can really hold weight."

Supreme cracked his knuckles. "When do we talk retaliation?"

Genesis met his eyes. "Soon. We definitely making our move before the end of the week."

"Perfect," Supreme smiled.

"But we also need to clear the rats in our own house," Genesis added.

The room went still again.

"We've got a mole," Genesis said flatly. "Someone fed info about our warehouse schedule last month. Caleb flagged inconsistencies."

Caleb tapped the screen again, pulling up texts and call logs. "We can't confirm who yet, but someone's bleeding intel to Maverick's people."

Genesis nodded toward Precious. "Double security protocol. Anyone late on check-ins gets blacklisted until verified. And start monitoring *everyone*. Phones. Bank statements. The whole nine."

"I'll take care of it," Precious said. No hesitation.

Genesis's voice lowered. "I want to know who sold us out. And when I do..." He didn't finish the sentence. He didn't have to.

Silence followed, charged and heavy. Supreme broke the stillness, his voice dropping to a whisper.

"When we strike, it's just us in this room pulling triggers. No outsiders, no lieutenants. That way our rat can' t warn nobody."

Genesis' eyes narrowed as he nodded. "Silent circle. It's family only. Core team. I'm with that." His eyes moved from face to face. Around the table, heads dipped in solemn agreement.

Then Genesis turned to Caleb. "Now that you handled the Shiffon situation, when the time is right, I'll divulge that information to Maverick and send him spinning. Let's see how he handles losing a child."

Caleb's spine straightened. "Yeah," he said. He dropped his gaze to the table. Didn't say another word.

Genesis looked at each of them in turn. "No mistakes. No mercy. The war already started. Time to make sure we finish it strong." Because in that room, war was already breathing.

Night draped Brooklyn in shadows, the kind that whispered secrets and swallowed screams. A battered depository sat quiet on the edge of East New York, its brick walls tagged and tired. Inside, two of Riot's men played spades, their laughter echoing between concrete pillars. They weren't expecting company. They never heard the black SUV roll up.

Supreme was first through the side entrance—silencer on, eyes like steel. Nico flanked the opposite side, cutting the power with a flick of his wrist. Darkness swallowed the building. The laughter stopped.

"Yo?!" one of the men called out.

His voice didn't make it to the end of the sentence.

A single *thump*—the sound of a body dropping. Supreme stepped over him, weapon still raised, breath steady.

On the far end, the second man bolted for the back, slipping on loose gravel. Nico caught him at the exit, gun leveled at the man's chest.

"Wait!" the man begged. "I was just watching the spot, I don't know—"

Nico pulled the trigger. No hesitation. No sermon. Just silence.

Outside, Caleb stood with the engine running, face tight. Precious was beside him, eyes on the building, fingers tapping the grip of her Glock like a metronome. She wasn't one for unnecessary body counts—but tonight wasn't about discretion. It was about dominance.

Supreme exited first, unbothered, rolling his neck like he just finished a workout. Nico followed, wiping blood from his knuckles with a handkerchief embroidered with his initials. They got in the SUV without a word.

"You leave a calling card?" Precious asked from the back.

Nico grinned, pulling out a folded piece of paper. "Left it on the body."

Caleb raised an eyebrow. "What was it?"

Nico tossed the paper back toward him. A cigar band. Black and gold. Caleb read the message scrawled inside.

"Harlem sends its regards."

"Let Riot know we ain't just playing defense anymore," Supreme scoffed.

Caleb pulled the SUV into traffic without turning on the headlights. Genesis's voice buzzed in his head as they drove. *We don't wait. We push back.* Tonight, they pushed hard. And now?

Now they waited for the scream to echo back. The SUV slid through the night, a black ghost on the streets of Brooklyn. Caleb kept his eyes on the road, hands gripping the steering wheel like it was the only thing keeping him tethered. Beside him, Precious was a statue of ice, her gaze fixed on the side mirror, watching the depository shrink into the distance. The cigar band sat on the center console; the message scrawled inside still fresh. *"Harlem sends its regards."* A fuckin' calling card, like this was some old-school mob shit. But that was Nico—always adding a touch of that old Harlem flair.

Caleb could feel the tension in the car, thick and choking. Supreme sat behind him, a wall of silent rage. Nico was a coiled snake, ready to strike at the slightest provocation. And Precious... she was something else. Quiet, calculating. He could feel the sweat trickling down his back, sticking his shirt to his skin. The SUV's air conditioning was blasting, but it did little to cool the heat of what they'd just done. He imagined the shocked expressions of Riot's men as they fell, the way their bodies crumpled like rag dolls. It was a necessary evil, a message that needed sending, but it sat heavy in his gut.

As they sped through the night, Brooklyn turned to Manhattan, the boroughs merging into a seamless sprawl of concrete and steel. Caleb knew these streets like the back of his hand, every alley, every shortcut, every hideaway. But tonight, they felt unfamiliar, like a stranger's territory.

He glanced at Precious out of the corner of his eye. She was staring straight ahead, her profile etched against the city lights. There was a tension in her jaw, a tightness that told him she was processing, calculating. He wanted to ask her what she was thinking, but the words stuck in his throat. Instead, he kept his eyes on the road. This was the world they operated in, no remorse. Just cold efficiency.

Chapter Seven

Quiet Before Chaos

Candlelight flickered across the polished wood of the private dining table, casting soft shadows on the walls of the intimate Harlem bistro. Kyra smiled across the table, her chin resting lightly in her palm, a single gold and diamond bracelet catching the light as she reached for her wine.

"You apologized with this beautiful bracelet after you had to leave in the middle of our dinner date a few weeks ago. Tonight is my turn to make things right," Kyra said, fingertips brushing her wrist. "That hospital emergency call pulled me away the other night. But trust me, all I wanted to do was stay."

Nico studied her over the rim of his glass, dark eyes lingering. "Life happens. But I ain't mad at the upgrade."

Kyra's dress hugged her curves just right—soft velvet the color of midnight. Her hair was slicked back into a sleek bun, the kind that left nothing to distract from her beauty. She laughed, her eyes playful. "So... this counts as an upgrade?"

"You? That view? That perfume?" Nico leaned forward, brushing his thumb across her hand. "Yeah. This definitely counts."

After dinner, they stepped into the chill of the night air. Nico's driver waited by the curb; door already open. Kyra hesitated only for a second before sliding in beside him.

Back at Nico's place, any apprehension, uncertainty, or shared adrenaline built up throughout the night-melted away as soon as they crossed the threshold of his loft. The building loomed large, the exterior was a mix of brick and steel, with large industrial windows that gleamed in the city lights. The entrance was grand, with intricate carvings adorning a double door made of dark wood and iron detailing, and a sleek modern lobby inside. The scent of aged wood and brick mingled with the sweet smell of expensive candles burning inside the loft, creating an intoxicating aroma.

Nico's loft mirrored the man himself—hard exterior, unexpected opulence within. Raw industrial bones dressed in luxury's skin. Exposed brick walls showcased million-dollar art pieces while Italian leather furniture sat atop polished concrete floors. The space told his story without words: street soldier turned empire lieutenant. But as the door clicked shut behind them, the carefully curated atmosphere faded to background noise. Their eyes locked across the room, a silent current passing between them, desire on a tight leash, neither was willing to break first. From hidden speakers, bass notes throbbed low, matching the rhythm of their heartbeats.

Kyra slipped out of her heels, leaving them at the door. Nico's gaze followed her movements, lingering, his collar suddenly too tight against his throat.

"You need another drink?" he asked, voice rougher than he intended.

Kyra released her hair from its sleek bun, dark waves cascading past her shoulders. She crossed the room without hesitation, deliberate in every step. "I need you instead."

The space between them vanished. His mouth found hers, hungry and certain. One hand gripped her waist, the other lost itself in her hair. They crashed through the space, shedding everything that separated them—jacket, shirt, cufflinks, then the thin layer of fear that neither wanted to name. Each piece of clothing dropped was a line crossed, a rule burned, until Nico barely recognized himself, and he knew Kyra felt the same by the way she clung tighter with every step. They staggered through the living room, laughing, breathless, as they nearly took out a glass sculpture on the coffee table. Nico pulled her back before it shattered, the reckless edge of their dance making every heartbeat louder in his chest. They left a trail of discarded clothing from living room to bedroom.

By the time they collapsed onto his bed, Nico was stripped down to something closer to the kid he used to be—a little scared, a lot desperate, and totally unprepared for how much this would mean. Kyra's hands mapped scars he'd stopped cataloguing, her mouth traced the faded lines, the bullet wounds, the knife marks. She wasn't asking for explanations, just memorizing him, the way a person does when they suspect it might not last yet praying it does. Nico gripped her hips, guiding her over him, and for once, let himself break the pattern of control he lived by. He let her set the pace, the rhythm, the violence of it and the sudden, aching tenderness when she cupped his jaw, kissed him soft, and where whispers replaced words. The loft's city lights bled in through the windows, painting their bodies in streaks of gold and blue that made everything look cinematic, epic, destined.

Afterward, Kyra's head rested against his chest, their breathing fell into rhythm. Nico remained silent, clinging to whatever peace he could find. He wasn't sure if it would last. But he'd remember this-her, here, him, whole-for as long as he could. He let himself breathe. Let himself feel. Let himself hope, just for a little longer. Nico didn't know if that made him weak or strong. It made him human. And for the first time in too damn long, that felt like enough. He continued to stay quiet, but his arms tightened around her, betraying what he couldn't voice—that his fortress walls had finally been breached.

Across the river, at their estate in New Jersey sat perched on a stony rise-a modernist wedge of glass and stone, lit from within and surrounded by winter-stripped oaks that creaked in the cold wind. It was a fortress designed for tranquility, meant to keep the world at bay, but tonight, inside the living room, there was a kind of closeness that made the whole structure feel less like a barricade and more like a sanctuary.

The mood was quieter but just as intimate. Supreme and Precious had retreated here after a day that clung to their skin, a day that left bruises invisible but real. They sat in their living room, the fire throwing reflections across the lines of their faces. A rare vintage bottle of champagne between them and the warmth of their fireplace dancing in their eyes. Her legs draped across his lap, and he was absently tracing circles on her ankle.

"You realize we've been running nonstop since this war started," Precious said, her voice a low current, sipping from her flute. "Not one real night off. Not for us, not for anybody."

Supreme, who'd been staring into the fire with his mind elsewhere, nodded and set the bottle down, pouring her another glass before refilling his own. "Tell me about it," Supreme agreed. "I miss us. Just us. You know when we last ate a meal without a phone on the table?"

She smiled, but it was a tired smile, the kind worn by those who know the odds are never really in their favor. "I miss us too," Precious said, letting her head drift to his shoulder. The simple contact grounded her, made the estate's scale feel less hollow. "Once this thing with Maverick is done, and Genesis is good... I want us to disappear for a minute. Somewhere far. Somewhere soft."

Supreme kissed her forehead. "Say less. I already got my eye on a spot in Turks, private cove, big ass infinity pool. the works. We take a jet. I lose the phone for a week and see if we still remember how to be people." He continued tracing circles on her ankle, the rhythm as steady and subtle as the pulse in his own wrist. "I keep thinking, once this all shakes out—when we finally put Maverick in a fuckin' box—we're done. We just... stop for a while. Hit the brakes. I want to remember what it feels like to not be looking over my shoulder."

He expected his wife to push back, but Precious just nodded, her eyes half-lidden as she stared at the flames.

"Just me and you?" she asked.

"Yes, just me and you."

Precious closed her eyes and let the dream

build itself: the two of them on white sand, sea grappling for their toes, the only urgency being how long it took the sun to set. "You'd actually last a week?" she teased, nudging his thigh with her foot. "I give you three days, tops. You'll start plotting a comeback within an hour."

Supreme grinned, but the edge had dulled. "Maybe. But I'd rather plot it with you. Just you."

For a while, the only sound was the snapping of the fireplace and the distant rumble from outside. Precious let herself drift, the tension in her muscles uncoiling one knot at a time. Although she was born, bred, and came up in the grimy Brooklyn streets, she'd never told Supreme how close she'd come, back in the early days, to just walking away. The violence, the constant threat, it was a hell of a thing. But Supreme had always been her gravity; the one thing she couldn't break orbit from. Sometimes she wondered if he knew that, if he understood how much of her survival was tied to his.

Supreme leaned back, stretching his arms across the top of the sofa, careful not to disrupt the space they'd conjured. In another lifetime, they'd be boring: a couple drinking good liquor by the fire, talking about vacations. But here, every moment of peace was a rebellion. Every minute they weren't preparing for war was a minute stolen from the chaos outside.

A log in the hearth split with a crack, sending up a burst of sparks. Precious watched them rise, then turned to Supreme. "Think we'll ever have a normal life?" she asked, her tone half-joke, half-wound.

Supreme's reply was immediate, as if he'd rehearsed it in his head a hundred times. "Fuck normal," he said, and there was a kind of nostalgia in it, like he was remembering a time before the world got complicated. "Normal is for people who don't know what it costs. We got something better. We got us."

Precious considered this, then nodded. She'd never admit it out loud, but that was the answer she needed—because it meant that the pain had a purpose, and that she wasn't alone in it.

A sudden ping broke the silence—his phone, lighting up with a message. Supreme checked it, frowned, then set it face down on the table, refusing to let it drag them back into the darkness just yet.

"Crisis?" she said, eyebrow raised.

"Can wait till morning," Supreme replied, and he meant it. There was nothing tonight that couldn't keep until the daylight.

They sat in a silence that was less absence and more communion, the kind of quiet that fills itself with unspoken promises. As the fire burned lower, the champagne bottle emptied, and the city beyond the glass faded to a murmur, Supreme and Precious let themselves be held by the moment—two souls battered but unbroken, finding shelter in each other as the storm raged on outside.

But peace was short-lived. A thousand miles south, where the air tasted of salt and the dolphins taunted jet skiers just offshore, Maverick's private fortress sat perched above the ocean's edge. Everything about the hideout was engineered for power: the armored glass, the hurricane-proof shutters, the razor-wire fencing buried in hibiscus hedges. But at the center of it all, Maverick himself was the real barricade—a man built of bone and rage, and lately, too much Red Bull.

He paced the marble floor barefoot, pale scars knotting his otherwise flawless calves and shins. The sun had just set, sky bleeding orange into indigo, but Maverick's mood was pure static.

Surveillance monitors lined the far wall, reflecting glare onto his angular face as he watched, again and again, the security footage from Houston. Each loop showed the same: black-clad figures moving with military precision, breaching a reinforced door, tossing smoke grenades, torching his stash house to the concrete.

He didn't even notice Riot until the man was halfway through his Cuban cigar, leaning against the kitchen's steel island, eyes bored but alert.

"You think this is funny?" Maverick barked, voice echoing in the cavernous great room.

"Not funny," Riot replied, blowing a ring of smoke toward the ceiling. "Just impressive. Genesis finally got the balls to make some legit moves. Brooklyn now Houston. Nigga been busy. I kinda respect that."

Maverick's fist slammed down on the glass coffee table. The sound was surgical knife through cartilage. The surface didn't just shatter, it exploded, shards skimming across the floor like ice on a pond. Riot didn't even flinch, but his smile widened.

Maverick stalked over, jaw twitching. "They hit the Houston house like it was nothing. Burned the product. Took the cash. Left a message on the back wall: This is chess. Your king's next."

Now Riot's smile faded. He dropped the cigar onto the tile, ground it out with his heel. "They're pokin' the bear. We can't let that slide."

Maverick's breath stuttered, the only tell he'd ever let slip. He was thinking—not the hot, impulsive kind, but the cold arithmetic that came just before someone died. He moved to the kitchen, poured a double of bourbon, and downed it in a single swallow.

"We don't let it slide," he said quietly, as if testing the idea against the silence. "We escalate."

Riot followed, arms crossed, black t-shirt stretched tight across his chest. "You want to level Houston?"

Maverick shook his head. "Let them think they've won that round. The next move isn't Houston. It's New York. We cut the legs out from under them before they can even celebrate."

He grabbed his phone, punched speed dial. It rang once before an answer—Tomo, Miami's local enforcer, the closest thing Maverick had to a priest.

"Genesis made his play," Maverick said. "I want eyes everywhere north of I-10. Nobody moves in or out of the city without me hearing about it. And get me the locations of Genesis's safe houses in the Bronx and Brooklyn. Every last one."

He hung up before Tomo could answer, turned back to Riot. "We start leaking rumors tonight. Make them think the retaliation will come from the cartels, or the Russians, or whoever the fuck else has a grudge. Smoke and mirrors."

Riot grinned, showing a chipped canine. "Love a good ghost story."

Maverick started pacing again, hands behind his back. "And then we do the real work. Kidnap the right person, torch the right spot, make a statement so loud even the Feds blink. I want Genesis to feel it in his teeth."

Riot's eyes lit up. "You got someone in mind?"

A pause. Maverick tapped a rhythm on his own forearm, a nervous habit leftover from a childhood in juvie. "Maybe that chick Pilar who works for Genesis's sister. Or you remember the kid from New Rochelle, the one who used to run numbers for Genesis before he got sent upstate? What was his name—Deshawn? He's out on parole now. Fat, lazy, soft. But his cousin's still in the game."

Riot's grin widened. "You want me to hit the cousin?"

"Not yet." Maverick's voice dropped to a whisper. "I want you to turn him. Quietly. Make it look like he came crawling to us for protection.

If we play it right, we can smoke out every weak link in Genesis's circle before we even fire a shot. If that don't work, we go the Pilar route next."

Riot nodded. "You want me to reach out?"

"Tonight."

Riot slipped out, already pulling up contacts on a burner phone.

Maverick stood in the center of the ruined living room, glass underfoot, bourbon burning his stomach raw. He stared at the security feed one last time, froze it on the last frame: a can of black spray paint, still dripping, the threat on the wall glistening in the floodlights.

He didn't just want to win. He wanted the other side to understand, viscerally, what it cost to challenge him.

For a moment, he closed his eyes and saw a younger version of himself—skinny, bruised, locked in a group home with thirty other broken boys, all of them fighting for the last scrap of anything. He'd promised himself back then that nobody would ever make him feel small again. Not Genesis, not the cops, not even the ghosts of everyone he'd put in the ground.

He opened his eyes. Took another drink. The plan was already forming in his head: an attack in New York that would force Genesis to react, to show his hand, maybe even draw him out into the open. It was surgical. It was personal. And it was already in motion.

He called his fixer in Manhattan, gave the order: Tomorrow night. Same time, same street. Make sure they see it coming.

The line went dead, and for the first time all day, Maverick smiled.

Chapter Eight

War Games

The morning sun cut low across the South Carolina horizon, bathing the hidden estate in gold. Spanish moss clung to the trees like secrets, and the wind whispered through the porch screens. The location was untraceable—off-grid, heavily secured, the kind of place you vanished into, not escaped from.

Genesis stepped out of the black SUV, nodding to the armed guard at the gate. His expression softened only when he saw her—Talisa, standing barefoot in the doorway, their daughter clutched at her hip. Her curls were wild, eyes just like Amir's—bright, curious, already carrying the burden of a name she'd one day learn was written in blood.

"Baby," Talisa breathed, stepping forward.

Genesis met her halfway, scooping his daughter into his arms before wrapping Talisa in a one-armed hug. For a moment, he let himself breathe. Let himself feel. Because this was the part he was fighting for—the laughter that echoed through living rooms, the smell of pancakes on Sunday mornings. Family.

Precious's SUV pulled up quietly behind his. She stepped out in black joggers and an olive-green trench, makeup light, hair tied back. She offered a soft smile as she approached the porch.

"Talisa," Precious greeted warmly. "You're glowing. That's either the sunlight or a top-secret skincare routine I need to know about."

Talisa laughed, her voice easing some of the tension in Genesis's chest. "Please, girl. Just a whole lot of peace and no stress—except when my husband forgets to call."

Precious raised an eyebrow at Genesis and smiled. "I'll make sure he's held accountable. Maybe over dinner once this war is over."

Talisa nodded. "It's a date."

They embraced briefly, the kind of hug women gave when words were unnecessary. Precious excused herself and made her way back to the SUV, giving the couple privacy.

Genesis watched her go before turning to Talisa. He took her hand in his.

"She's become your second wife," Talisa said suddenly, the words soft, but pointed.

"You know she's just a close friend. Always has been. But I won't lie—she's stepped up in ways I didn't see coming. I've needed her. She's helped keep everything from falling apart," Genesis admitted.

Talisa looked at him, eyes searching. "And what about us?"

He stepped in closer, cupping her face. "You are my *only* wife. Don't get it twisted. Precious is loyal, ride-or-die—but you? You're my air. My peace. My future. Nobody could ever take that from you. Besides, you know everything you are to me, is what Precious is to Supreme. They locked in, just like us."

She nodded, eyes glistening. He kissed her forehead, then her lips—slow, lingering, like a promise he meant to keep. Their daughter tugged at his sleeve, and he picked her up one last time, nuzzling her cheek before passing her back to Talisa.

"I'll be back," he said.

"You better be," Talisa replied.

He turned and walked toward the SUV; the door already open. Precious was inside, flipping through a thick manila folder filled with notes, addresses, and intel. She looked up when he slid in beside her.

"Ready to brief Renny?" she asked.

Genesis fastened his seatbelt. "Yeah. Let's bring Houston up to speed."

The jet streaked across a cloudless sky, touching down just past noon, wheels kicking up heat off the tarmac. Houston's skyline shimmered in the distance like a mirage—glossy towers and sprawling streets, beautiful but boiling underneath. The pilot taxied to the far side of the private terminal, away from prying eyes, where a pair of blacked-out SUVs idled behind a chain-link fence. Genesis pressed his forehead to the window, scanning for threats even before the plane stopped moving. Years in the game had taught him: the only place to let your guard down was six feet under.

Precious stepped onto the private runway, both dressed in muted tones, their energy sharp and focused. She was already up, trench coat draped over her forearm, phone buzzing in her palm. Every alert made her flinch—a rare tell that Genesis took as a warning sign. She caught his eye and shrugged, using her thumb to dismiss a notification before shouldering her duffel bag.

On the tarmac, the heat rose in visible waves, blurring the soldiers in tactical gear who swept the area. Genesis gave them a nod as he and Precious made their way down the steps and toward the waiting armored SUV. The driver, a local affiliate named Javier, opened the door without a word.

Inside was air-conditioned darkness. Renny sat sprawled in the rear-facing seat, sneakers propped on a fold-out ottoman, cigar burning low and slow between his fingers. His face was blank, but his posture was loose—like a man holding a winning hand and waiting to see if anyone else noticed. His eyes flicked between Genesis and Precious like he already knew war was trailing behind them. Genesis climbed in first, letting his eyes adjust to the dimness.

"Long time," Renny said as they climbed in.

"Not long enough," Genesis replied, giving

him a firm dap. Precious slid in behind them and closed the door.

As the SUV merged onto the freeway, the city unfolded in glass and granite, cranes silhouetted against a sky so bright it looked fake. They drove in silence for a stretch, the only sound the hum of the engine and the low thump of bass from a passing car.

Genesis watched the city slide by through the tinted window. "Feel like Houston's the only place left where I can move in daylight," he remarked.

Renny grinned. "That's 'cause I keep it that way."

Precious leaned forward, eyes cutting to the cigar. "You hear about Philly last night?"

Renny nodded. "Eight bodies. Two kids."

Genesis's jaw flexed. "Maverick's calling cards. He's not even hiding it anymore. And now Riot's in the mix."

Finally, the SUV turned onto a side street, then pulled into an underground garage beneath an unmarked building. Genesis clocked the security—cameras, motion sensors, a kill box at the entrance. Renny had stepped up his game.

In the elevator, nobody spoke. When they reached the top floor, it looked nothing like an office. Inside, they gathered in a sleek conference room outfitted with multiple screens, digital maps, and a long table that had seen too many emergency meetings. It was more like a bunker— conference table bolted to the floor, touchscreen panels embedded in the walls, stocked bar in one corner. Renny poured himself a bourbon, then gestured for the others to join him at the table.

He flicked the cigar into a glass tray. "We got a lot to cover. People been sniffing around my warehouses. Rumor is, Riot Mercer had his people moving in through Third Ward. And I know for a fact two of my spots got hit last week."

Genesis stood, arms folded, while Precious opened a laptop and slid it toward Renny. Images flickered across the screen—burned-out stash houses, Riot Mercer captured mid-laugh on a gas station camera, footage of Pilar narrowly escaping the botched abduction attempt.

"We traced the attacks. Maverick's using burner crews, but they all source back to a shell company in Pearland. Maverick's getting sloppier," Precious said. "But Riot? He's young and hungry. Demon energy. He wants to make a name for himself—wants to outshine Cortez, make the Mercer name mean something again."

"Problem is," Genesis added, "he don't care

who gets caught in the fire. Innocents. Women. Kids. He's got no rules."

"Your security's tight, but someone inside's leaking shipment data," Precious added.

Renny's face hardened. "You think it's Javier?"

Genesis shook his head. "Javier's solid. We checked his people. This is bigger than an inside job—it's a network. They're pulling city permits, tracking your deliveries, maybe even hacking into your suppliers."

Renny sipped bourbon and stared at the screen, then at Genesis. "You didn't come all this way to tattle on my security."

"No," Genesis said. "We need to coordinate. Maverick's not just trying to squeeze you—he's building something. A coalition. Pilar was spotted in Miami last week, deep in talks with the Vasquez cartel. Then that same night, Cortez's enforcers started popping up in Dallas. If we don't get ahead of this, we're all on the menu."

The room went quiet except for the hum of the AC.

Renny broke the silence. "So, what's the play?"

Genesis leaned in. "We hit one of their warehouses. Clean. Precise. But retaliation is coming.

We expect it. You and your crew gotta stay sharp. This thing ain't just East Coast anymore."

Renny nodded slowly. "I already tightened up security around my people. Genevieve included."

That name hung in the air like smoke.

Precious exchanged a glance with Genesis before saying, "We haven't fully brought her into the loop yet."

Renny's brow lifted. "Why? She's tougher than half the hitters you brought today."

Genesis's jaw tightened. "Because once she's in, there's no walking it back. And right now, her attention's still on rebuilding The Garden Room, expanding her business. She knows Cortez is dead. But if she finds out Maverick's still aiming at our heads..."

"She might go nuclear," Renny finished for him.

"That's why we need her focused," Genesis said. "Not blinded by revenge. Not unless it's a last resort."

Renny exhaled through his nose. "Now what?"

Precious brought up a map of the city, red dots fanned out along the I-610 Loop. "Tomorrow at 3:17 PM, this warehouse gets a shipment from the Gulf. We know Maverick's people plan to intercept. We let them take it—then hit the spot when they're sorting product. Clean, decisive, but big enough to send a message."

Renny considered. "How many bodies?"

"None, if we do it right," Genesis said. "We want to scare them, not start another war."

Renny nodded, but his eyes were already calculating. "Who's on the team?"

"Me. Precious. Nico, if he makes it in time. We need one of your guys for local backup."

Renny gave a short laugh. "You don't trust my people, but you want them to ride shotgun?"

Genesis shrugged. "Trust is earned. Besides, I'm not here for a reunion. I just want this to end."

Renny leaned back, bourbon in hand. "What about me?"

"You're the decoy," Precious said. "You show up at a club across town, make a scene, draw the lookouts away from the warehouse. Maverick's got eyes everywhere, but he's still obsessed with you. Use that."

Renny smiled, the old cockiness returning. "I can do that."

They spent the next hour dissecting the plan, running through contingencies, debate escalating in tense, clipped exchanges. Every scenario ended the same: Maverick gaining ground, unless they took a risk. Finally, Genesis stood up and paced to the window, staring down at the city.

"Why does this feel like a losing fight?" he asked quietly.

Precious answered without looking up. "Because we're playing defense. And Maverick? He's playing chess with matches."

Renny stood too, finishing his bourbon. "Time to flip the board."

He walked over and put a hand on Genesis's shoulder. "You know, if we pull this off, Houston's yours. Full stop. Nobody will come for you again."

Genesis gave a thin smile. "I'll believe it when I see it."

A message buzzed on Precious's phone. She read it, then closed the laptop. "Nico's landed. He's enroute."

Genesis straightened his jacket. "Let's go."

They took the elevator back down, silence thick but purposeful. Javier opened the SUV door. This time, Genesis noticed the subtle bulge at his waistband—a Glock, safety off. Even the drivers were on edge.

As they navigated the labyrinth of Houston's streets, Precious checked her phone, then Genesis's. "Next right, then one block up," she said. "Nico's waiting in the alley." She then received another text from one of her trusted sources. It was an address to a home where answers waited. She relayed the info to Javier, as it would be the next stop after picking up Nico.

They found him leaning against a dumpster, phone pressed to his ear, face pinched with worry. He hung up when he saw them, jogging over with a soldier's stride.

"Nico," Precious said, "you get the files?"

He nodded. "And more. Maverick's crew is doubling their numbers. They're making a play tomorrow night, not afternoon. Intel was a diversion—the real target is the distribution hub in The Heights."

"Muthafuckers," Renny grunted.

Genesis shot Precious a look. "You still got that secondary team on standby?"

She smiled grimly. "Always."

There was a quick, whispered debate in Spanish between Nico and Javier, then Nico turned to Genesis.

"We hit The Heights first. Maverick won't expect it. But we'll need at least two more shooters."

"I'll get them," Renny said, already texting.

They sped off toward the address, every mile stripping away the illusion of safety. Genesis checked his own gun, then rolled his neck, the tension never leaving his eyes.

Precious reached over and touched his wrist. "We'll get through this. We always do."

He didn't answer, but the look he gave her said everything.

The SUV pulled up to a nondescript row house, old but well-kept. A battered sedan sat parked across the street, engine off but taillights still hot. Nico got out first, scanning the area, then motioned for the others.

Inside, it was dark and spare—bare floors, the sound of a fridge whirring in the background. Nico led them to a back room, where a whiteboard was covered with names and pictures. The room felt tight, like a cell, the air thick with the scent of old coffee and cigarette smoke. Nico's voice echoed off the bare walls as he laid out the plan, his words clipped and precise. Genesis listened, his gaze flicking between the whiteboard and the faces around him. Precious stood close, her presence a silent support, but her eyes were all business. She was already three steps ahead, calculating, strategizing. Renny leaned against the wall, arms crossed, a grim smile on his face.

He was ready for this—too ready.

Genesis could feel the weight of their expectations, the pressure of the clock ticking down. He looked at the faces on the whiteboard, committing each one to memory. Maverick's lieutenants, Riot's associates, even a few cops who were dirty enough to be on the payroll. Each one a target, each one a step closer to dismantling Maverick's sprawling web.

His eyes lingered on Riot's image—the kid's smirk was a taunt, a promise of chaos yet to come. He could almost hear the tick of a clock in his head, counting down to the moment when this would all explode. Genesis could see the threads, the weak points where they could cut deep. He traced the lines with his eyes, each possibility unfolding like a deck of cards in his mind. The streets had taught Genesis one truth: in this game, second place meant a casket, and he wasn't ready for his yet.

Chapter Nine

Pressure Points

Pilar stepped out of the back of the Escalade, stilettos clicking against the cracked concrete as she adjusted her sunglasses and scanned the parking lot. The Houston humidity clung to her like perfume, but she barely noticed. She was back, reluctantly—but with purpose. Miami had been business. Serious business. She'd just finished negotiating a short-term distribution deal with one of the city's smaller cartels—legit money, clean hands, at least on paper. It wasn't glamorous, but it was a power play. One she hoped would elevate her game and her reputation beyond Houston's shadowy corridors.

But something felt...off.

She entered the back hallway of the boutique office suite Genevieve had gifted her access to and paused. The hallway lights buzzed faintly. She turned back just in time to catch the silhouette of a man disappear behind a building across the street.

Her phone buzzed. Unknown number. She declined it. Then it buzzed again. This time, a message.

Welcome home.

She stiffened. The last person who said that to her was dead. Pilar glanced both ways, pushed into the suite, and locked the door behind her.

What she didn't know—couldn't know—was that Riot Mercer had been tracking her since her Miami departure. Maverick had wanted her snatched up as a way to spook Genevieve into making reckless moves, maybe even luring her out. But Pilar was harder to corner than they expected. She changed routines, worked in silence, and had street instincts that couldn't be taught.

The kidnapping attempt failed before it started. One of Riot's men tried to follow her from the airport but ended up concussed in a hotel dumpster by the time Pilar was done with him. Riot watched the footage later with a smirk.

"She's sharper than they said," he muttered. "Might have to handle her myself."

Justina sat in her SUV outside the private preschool where little Desi spent his mornings. Her fingers tapped against the steering wheel; her eyes locked on the entrance. She wasn't sure if she was watching for her son or for Dominique.

Things with Desmond had gotten... complicated. Again. They had fallen back into each other like gravity, like a habit too old to break. But love wasn't simple, not with Dominique hovering in the background, always calculating, always bitter.

Dominique was the most insidious kind of rival, the sort who played the long game and never lost her temper. She'd earned her PhD from the concrete corners, collecting street wisdom no university could teach. Her hustle was pure instinct—the kind that turned nothing into something, that transformed desperation into strategy. And in this game? That education was deadlier than any Ivy League connections. She wore her hair natural, always glossed and sculpted, and her Instagram grid was a masterclass in understated flexing. It made Justina sick, the way Desmond still talked about her, never with scorn but always with a sigh. As if Dominique's calculated seduction was just some innocent misstep instead of the deliberate chess move Justina knew it to be.

And worse, she had a child with Desmond—a girl Justina didn't blame but found hard to accept. She was a reminder of her ex-husband's betrayal. The worst pain.

Justina couldn't bring herself to resent the little girl, especially watching how Desi's face lit up whenever his baby sister toddled into the room. But Dominique wasn't satisfied with just co-parenting. When Justina had married Amir, she had seen her path clear—she would step into the vacancy and become the next Mrs. Blackwell. Now with Amir gone, Justina caught those calculating glances, that slight tilt of Dominique's chin whenever Desmond's name came up. That smile—barely there but unmistakable—that whispered: "You had your chance."

Her latest move? Enrolling her daughter at Desi's exclusive preschool—-a place with a two-year waiting list that somehow made room the moment Dominique mentioned her connection to the Blackwell name. "For the siblings to bond," she'd explained with those doe eyes and a sugar-sweet smile. And Desmond, ever the optimist, ate that bullshit up, blind to the calculated positioning that Justina saw clear as day, and it made her blood simmer. While everyone else scrambled for their next move, Dominique had already mapped out the board ten steps ahead. She didn't just want visitation rights or child support payments. She wanted the keys to the kingdom.

Justina caught herself grinding her molars again. She sipped from her iced coffee, forcing her hands to unclench on the wheel. Calm, she told herself. You're better than this.

Today was just a routine pickup. She wasn't even supposed to be here; the housekeeper typically did the drop-offs and pickups while Justina worked at her "side business"—a high-end event-planning, that only barely turned a profit. But this morning she'd had a feeling, a little tap at the base of her skull, so she'd made an excuse, canceled a client meeting, and driven straight here, circling the block twice before parking. She kept looking for Dominique's car, a white Tesla with special chrome trim that gleamed like sharkskin. She hadn't seen it, but that didn't mean anything. Dominique could be anywhere.

So, Justina waited, watching the entrance, scrolling through her texts, checking Desmond's location (at the gym, as promised), and then scrolling again. She was deep into this cycle when the phone buzzed with a new message— Unknown Number.

She hesitated, then opened it: *Nice day, isn't it?*

She scanned the parking lot, peering through the dark tint. Nothing looked unusual. In Miami, every third car was an SUV, and most parents kept to themselves, eyes on their kids or their screens. Still, the message made her skin crawl.

Justina texted back, *Who is this?* The message was delivered, then left unread. She waited. Nothing.

Her finger hovered over Desmond's contact. No—he'd just overreact, insist she lock herself in the house with two guards posted at every entrance. The text was unsettling, but she wasn't ready to live like she had a target on her back. Not yet anyway.

What Justina didn't realize was that Dominique wasn't working alone. Her focus on Desmond's baby mama had blinded her to the other predators circling—ones with far deadlier intentions, the ones who saw her as more than a rival, but as prey.

She checked the rearview again and caught a flash of something in the side mirror: a nondescript black sedan, parked a little too far away, windows too dark. The driver's face was obscured by shadow and a ball cap, but she saw the camera—a long lens, pointed directly at her car.

Justina's heart stuttered. She turned the ignition off, grabbed her purse, and forced herself to step out, all business. She walked to the school's front door, heels loud on the concrete, trying to project confidence even as her nerves rattled. She signed in at the office, forced a smile at the woman behind the desk, and waited, back straight, for Desi to come out.

He appeared holding hands with a teacher, marshmallow cheeks smeared with paint, eyes lighting up at the sight of his mother. "Mommy!!" He ran to her, and she scooped him up, breathing in his familiar scent. She held him a little tighter than usual.

Justina forced herself not to look back at the black sedan as she crossed the lot. She bundled Desi into the car seat, buckled him in with deliberate care, then slid back behind the wheel. The sedan was gone. Had it even been there? She started the engine, hands trembling, and told herself: This is how Dominique would want you to act. Scared. On edge. She's not going to get to you. Not this time.

But the truth was, Justina was scared. Terrified, even. And if Dominique really was playing dirty, what else was she capable of? She drove home in silence, Desi singing softly in the back seat, and tried to ignore the persistent feeling that she was being watched. Maybe she was. But Justina wasn't the only one on edge.

Less than a mile away, the blacked-out Lincoln idled near a strip mall, its driver pulling off his cap and inserting a Bluetooth earpiece. He sent the day's photos—Justina at the wheel, Justina at the front office, Justina holding her child—straight to a secure folder accessible only by Maverick and his most trusted circle. Then he called the number he'd been given for the next phase of the operation.

"Target is exactly as you described," he said, voice toneless. "She's anxious. We'll keep the pressure up."

He hung up, put the car in drive, and disappeared into midmorning traffic.

At Maverick's Miami fortress he perused the latest batch of surveillance. He sat behind a desk of glass and steel, a smoldering Cohiba clenched between his fingers, the room smoky and cold despite the subtropical sun pounding the windows. Across from him, Riot Mercer waited, arms folded, face unreadable.

"She's predictable," Maverick said, flipping from photo to photo. "She wants to be the one in control, but fear is a language she understands. If we keep her guessing, she'll make a mistake. And then Desmond will have to pick a side."

Riot nodded but said nothing. He was a tool, not a strategist, and he knew it. Maverick enjoyed the silence, the power that came with it.

"Send Dominique the next set of instructions," Maverick said. "No mistakes this time. And make sure our friend at the preschool keeps a soft touch—Justina can't know we're behind this. Not yet."

Riot left to do as ordered, and Maverick leaned back, savoring the sharp burn of the cigar. He closed his eyes, conjuring the image of Justina's panic. The game was just beginning.

The television droned softly in the next room, reruns of *Martin* echoing in the quiet house.

Mia sat on the worn couch, foot bouncing, eyes darting to the hallway every few seconds. Her gaze flicked to the deadbolt on the front door as if she could will it to release and cough up the person they were both waiting for. She counted the seconds between each set of headlights that rolled past their block, then melted back into the suburban dark.

When the door finally groaned and popped, Mia's heart shot up into her throat. Even though she knew who it would be, she braced herself, because the Caleb who left in the morning was never quite the same as the one who returned at night. This version of him entered with a predator's caution—slipping inside before the storm door slammed, peeling his hoodie off with a practiced motion, duffel bag slung low like a weapon or a promise. For a split second, his eyes swept the room: first Mia, then the shadows behind her, then the corridor leading to the back room. Always, always, the back room.

"She asked about you again," Mia said, lobbing the sentence like a test. Her voice was more tired than angry, but she forced it to stay level, as though it might steady the trembling in her hands.

Caleb said nothing. He locked the door,

dropped the bag by the shoe rack, and scrubbed both palms down his face. With the hoodie off, the sharp lines of his jaw seemed harsher, the tired bruising under his eyes darker, almost theatrical. For a moment, he stood there in the tattered calm, breathing slow and deep, the way he used to center himself before stepping into a fight. Then he moved on, wordless.

Mia watched him cross to the kitchen, where he cracked open a bottle of water and chugged half of it, Adam's apple bobbing. She hated the way he ignored her, but hate was easier than admitting she was scared. She followed him, arms folded tight against her chest.

"Caleb," she said, more forcefully this time. "You can't keep pretending she's not back there. She's not a prisoner."

He finally met her eyes. His pupils were blown wide, adrenaline or something else, and when he spoke, his voice was raw, nearly a whisper. "She is if it keeps her alive."

Mia stared at him, dumbfounded by the cold logic. "You told Genesis she was dead."

He nodded, almost imperceptibly. "I had to."

"She's pregnant. What happens after she gives birth?" Her words came faster, sharper, like she was choking on each syllable.

Caleb looked away. "I haven't figured that part out yet."

Mia pressed both hands to her temples like she could squeeze sanity into her skull. "You're playing a dangerous game. If Genesis finds out—"

"We keep having this same conversation. I know what I'm doing." But the words landed flat, unconvincing, even to himself.

"No," Mia said, voice rising, "you're lying to everyone. Including yourself."

A silence ballooned between them, filled only by the TV's laugh track slipping around the corner. Mia wanted to shake him, to force him to see how desperate he'd become, but instead she just stood there, watching him sink onto the edge of the couch, elbows on knees, hands steepled.

In the back room, Shiffon floated in a slow, liminal fever. The smell of plywood and the faintest mildew clung to the air, not unpleasant but constant, like a reminder that nothing in this house was hers. She lay curled on her side, one hand splayed protectively over the rise of her belly, feeling the flutter and push of new life. It was the only thing she trusted: the fact that something inside her was growing, and that soon, somehow, it would have to come out.

She couldn't track time anymore. The windows in her room were papered over, letting in only the occasional wash of streetlight or the shiver of sirens from the main road. Sometimes, she lost herself in the memory of sunlight, the way it had once felt on her bare shoulders as a little girl running through the park.

Sometimes, she drifted back to that first night she met Caleb—his fingers tapping nervously against his glass, eyes darting away whenever she caught him staring. How his shoulders had softened when she leaned in and whispered, "You don't have to act tough in front of me," and the way his serious face had cracked into that rare, unguarded smile still lived somewhere behind her eyelids.

Now, she didn't see him much. He came to her only in brief, silent intervals—bringing food, standing in the doorway to check if she was breathing, then disappearing again. When he did talk, it was mostly to tell her what she couldn't do. Don't go near the front windows. Don't go outside. Don't make noise after midnight. The rules were simple, almost childish, but she followed them. Not because she believed in them, but because she hadn't yet figured out what the consequences would be if she broke them.

The last time he'd come in, he'd lingered at

the door for a long time, as if he was working up the nerve to say something. But in the end, he just left a new bottle of vitamins on the little table and told her, quietly, that he was sorry. She didn't know what he was sorry for.

Mia was a ghost: always present but never speaking to her directly. Shiffon had tried, once, to catch her eye as she carried laundry down the hall. But Mia had looked away, lips pressed together, face stone-set into a mask of professional detachment. Shiffon couldn't decide which was worse: the isolation, or the knowledge that someone out there who tried to kill her was now protecting her out of obligation, not love.

Tonight, she lay awake and listened to the rhythm of voices from the living room, the way Mia's rose and fell and Caleb's barely registered as a growl beneath it. She wondered what they were arguing about. Her? The baby? The fact that she was supposed to be dead?

Sometimes, in the dark, Shiffon entertained the idea that she really was dead, that Caleb had buried the old her somewhere in a field and this new, heavy, invisible person was all that remained. The thought made her laugh—quietly, so as not to break her own rules. The universe had a sick sense of humor—she'd gone from being the woman who put guns to heads and collected ransoms to becoming the prize in someone else's game of keep-away. Counting breaths, listening to footsteps, measuring freedom in square feet of a back bedroom.

In the living room, Caleb's shoulders hunched deeper. "I just want her to make it to delivery," he murmured, voice so low it barely carried. "After that... we'll figure out the rest."

In the back room, Shiffon pressed a palm to her belly, feeling the ripples of movement beneath the skin, and tried to picture what "the rest" might look like. Her thoughts drifted to Maverick, her baby's father, and a cold certainty settled in her chest. Whatever reunion might come—if it came at all—would be written in blood, not tears of joy.

Chapter Ten

Shot Callers

Back in New York, Genesis, Precious and Nico returned from Houston feeling victorious, while outside the rain hit the glass like war drums.

Genesis stood at the head of the long mahogany table inside his downtown war room—black walls, surveillance screens lining one side, a digital map of the tri-state area glowing in red and white pins. Supreme, Nico, Precious, and Caleb sat around him, each with that same restless energy: hungry, focused, dangerous.

"We poked the hornet's nest," Genesis said,

his voice low but sharp. "Now it's time to take the whole damn hive."

Nico leaned back in his seat, a toothpick rolling across his tongue. "Riot's out here moving reckless. That stash house hit we pulled, he ain't gon' let that slide."

"He shouldn't," Supreme said, arms crossed. "We wanted him loud. We wanted them reacting. Now they're exposed."

Caleb nodded, but there was a glint of something behind his eyes—buried deep. Only Precious caught it.

Genesis turned to him. "What's the word out of Philly?"

Caleb straightened. "Things are quiet. Word on the street is Shiffon skipped town. She's gone. Ghosted."

Satisfied—for now—Genesis turned his attention to the map. "Riot is gonna want to make a statement soon."

"Then we beat him to it," Precious said. "We hit their transportation hubs—cut off the money. Pressure the suppliers. Without product or profit, Riot becomes a liability. Maverick doesn't carry dead weight."

Nico smirked. "And what about Maverick?"

Genesis tapped the table. "He's playing long

game. Justina's in Miami. And don't think I don't know he's watching her."

"Desmond's back in the picture too," Supreme added. "He's moving like he owns her again."

Caleb frowned. "That could get messy."

"Already is," Precious said, pulling out her phone. "Justina don't even realize she's a pawn. We need eyes on her. If Maverick gets to her through Desmond, it's a wrap."

Genesis nodded. "I had eyes on her but I'm gonna put someone permanent. Quietly."

Then, he turned to the larger screen behind them and tapped a button. Surveillance footage from a corner in Brooklyn came up. A warehouse Riot had taken over. Trucks in and out. New faces, some familiar, some not. One, in particular, froze the room.

"Who's that?" Nico asked.

"Name's Kane. Former enforcer for Cortez," Genesis said. "Looks like Riot picked up the leftovers."

"You want him gone?" Supreme asked.

"Eventually. For now, I want to know who else is stepping up. Maverick's building something. And if we wait too long to dismantle it, we're gonna be fighting three heads instead of two."

The war room fell into silence. Then Precious stood.

"I'll have the intel team map out their routes and run financials on everyone tied to that warehouse."

"Good," Genesis said. "We keep squeezing until we force Maverick out of hiding or we get an exact location, so we can take him out."

Supreme stood next. "We need to prep the teams. Hit hard, hit fast, vanish."

Genesis nodded. Caleb hovered at the far end of the table as the others trickled out. Nico left first, the echo of his boots fading down the corridor. Supreme lingered longest, eyes flicking between Caleb and Genesis. Even Precious—who usually floated like the last leaf to fall—was gone before Caleb realized he and Genesis were alone.

Genesis didn't turn around, not yet. He let the silence sprawl, the only sound the faint hum of servers cooling themselves behind the black walls.

Caleb stood, unable to move, rehearsing every possible version of "She's gone" in his head. He willed his hands to unclench, but they didn't listen.

"Caleb." Genesis's voice cut through the static, more an order than a greeting.

Caleb straightened his jacket, stalling, and finally faced him. "Yeah?"

Genesis had already been staring—he must have been, the way his pupils seemed to dial in directly through Caleb's defenses. "Is there anything you think I should know about Shiffon?"

The question landed heavy, far heavier than when he'd ask about Shiffon in front of the group. Here, alone, it was a blade pressed gently to the jugular. "No. Nothing other than she's gone," Caleb repeated, the words almost convincing to his own ears. "Permanently."

Genesis studied him, motionless. "Funny thing about people who ghost, Caleb. Sometimes they're just waiting for a better signal." He let that hang, as if expecting Caleb to correct the record.

A drop of sweat traced down Caleb's hairline and into his collar. "Her trail ends on the bridge. She's gone, boss."

Genesis nodded, but there was no satisfaction in it. "You'll let me know if that changes."

Caleb shifted his weight, forcing steel into his voice. "She's gone, Genesis. Buried. My word is all I've ever had with you—and I'm giving it now."

Genesis's mouth curved just a millimeter. "Then I'll take you at your word."

The tension broke when Genesis dismissed him with a wave. Caleb pivoted to leave, but found himself frozen on the cold marble, his body betraying him before he could command it forward. He walked out of the war room each footstep echoed like a countdown. His chest tight, a reminder of the secret burning a hole in his gut. The weight of deception pressing against his ribcage. Genesis had given him everything—respect, purpose, family—and here he was, betraying it all. But the alternative haunted him worse: Shiffon's body, cold and still, her unborn child never drawing breath. Some sins even loyalty couldn't justify.

At the far end of the hallway, where the glow of the war room faded and the hum of overhead lights gave way to the hollow chill of the stairwell, Caleb finally let his lungs fill and empty. He pressed his palms to his knees and bent over, alone for the first time since the meeting began, the thudding of his heart finally outpacing the faint whine of surveillance cameras mounted above every door. For a second, he just stared at the polished concrete under his shoes, willing his stomach to settle. He straightened, wiped the sweat from his upper lip, forced his breathing even, and walked toward the fire exit instead of the elevator, letting the heavy door close behind him with a rush of cold air and the sharp tang of rainwater pooling on the city sidewalk outside.

On the landing, he hesitated. For months now, every exit felt like a trap door, every shadow a possible reckoning. The secret inside him warped his perception—he could feel it in the way his pulse reacted to the smallest change in temperature, or the way his muscles tensed when Genesis said his name. Deception was familiar territory, but this time the stakes eclipsed everything. Genesis discovering the truth meant more than just Caleb losing his rank—it meant his body would be found face down off the grid, if found at all.

Dominique sat on her plush white sectional, legs curled beneath her, a wine glass in hand, and bitterness bleeding from every pore. The penthouse was immaculate—marble floors, designer throw pillows, and melodic jazz playing in the background—but her toxic energy disrupted the elegance. She scrolled through Justina's IG story like she was flipping through a catalog of things that should've been hers. Baby Desi's face.

Desmond's arm in the background. Soft music playing. Candlelight.

She closed the app.

Her phone buzzed. Marcus. She smirked and opened the message.

Had her laughing tonight. Told her a story about my mom's peach cobbler and she lit up. She's comfortable around me now.

Dominique sipped her wine, letting the dryness cut across her tongue. She typed back:

Comfortable don't mean loyal. Keep pushing. Desmond's still in her bed.

A moment later, Marcus replied:

That's why I'm playing the friend card. She ain't expecting it. Told her I run a non-profit that helps single mothers build generational wealth. That got her attention.

Dominique rolled her eyes, but her lips curved.

Good. Keep pressing that angle. Now that she's a widow, Justina's flipped into trying to be this morally upright queen. Show her something Desmond never gave her—purpose. Let her start doubting him.

The typing bubble danced for a few seconds before Marcus answered:

You sure she's worth all this? I mean, Des-

mond already got a kid with you.

Dominique's entire body tensed. She set the wine glass down with a soft clink and called him instead.

He picked up immediately.

"You listen to me," she said, her voice like satin laced with venom. "That man might've given me a baby, but I'm trying to secure my future. Justina stole it from me once before and she's trying to do it again by running back into Desmond's arms like nothing happened. I'm not doing this for fun."

Marcus exhaled. "Alright. I get it."

"No," she snapped. "You don't. Not yet. But you will. And so will she. That fake fairytale they got going, it's ending. You're just the last chapter."

There was silence between them.

Then she added, soft now, almost seductive: "Do this right, Marcus... and I'll make sure *you* get something out of it too."

She hung up before he could respond.

In the quietness that followed, she lifted her wine glass to her lips, stepped onto the balcony, and let her gaze sweep across Miami's glittering skyline. Justina's downfall wouldn't be enough— Dominique needed to see her crawl, watch her plead for mercy that would never come. Between

Riot's muscle and Marcus's infiltration, she'd crafted the perfect trap. Not a question of if, but when. The thought warmed her more than the wine ever could.

Chapter Eleven

Fault Lines

Genevieve O'Neal closed the private lounge door behind her and pressed her back to the dark oak, letting her breath steady before she moved. The Garden Room was quiet—unnervingly so, the kind of eerie calm that always came before something catastrophic. Today, silence pressed in from every direction. Outside, clouds gathered like bruises over the Houston skyline, the city's usual heat dampened by the threat of rain. Inside, the air felt chilled, the kind of cold that wasn't about temperature but about what was coming.

Pilar stood by the window; her arms folded so tightly across her chest that the tendons trembled beneath her sleeves. She wore all black; even her lipstick was a shade of abyssal merlot. Her hair, normally wild and full of life, was scraped back in a severe bun. She stared through the glass, not at the view—the endless arterial tangle of I-10, the sprawl of glass towers and shopping complexes—but at her own reflection. When she finally turned, her face was a mask of nothing, except for the deepest set of shadows under her eyes.

"I appreciate you seeing me in person," Pilar said, voice barely more than a vibration.

Genevieve let herself drift off the door and crossed halfway into the room. "You said it was urgent." She scanned Pilar for wounds, for anxiety-tells: the way she kept shifting her weight, the slight tremor in her jaw.

"It is." Pilar swallowed. "I wouldn't call if it was nothing."

Genevieve nodded once. "It's good to see you, Pilar, but I have to admit, I didn't expect you back in Houston so soon, not after everything with Maverick, Cortez and what you endured from them orchestrating your kidnapping. Is that what this is about?"

Pilar's laugh was dry and humorless. "I wish it was about old shit. This is new." She looked away, and the muscles in her neck corded tight. "Somebody tried to snatch me again. Three times."

Genevieve didn't react, but she felt the shift inside her—a lowering of shields, a click of the mental rolodex. "Start from the beginning." She perched on the edge of the leather sofa, legs crossed, hands resting perfectly still in her lap.

Pilar exhaled through her nose, the window fogging just so. "First time was a couple weeks ago, right after I landed. I thought I was being paranoid when I saw the same black Suburban at the airport and then again at my hotel. But then, in the parking garage, two guys in masks tried to corner me. I ducked into the elevator, hit every floor, and lost them near the atrium. Security footage shows them, but their plates were covered. No prints, nothing."

Genevieve's fingers tightened just slightly on her knee. "Second time?"

"It had been awhile, but I stopped by the office space you let me use. I still had the key. Someone tried to come from me there. Then the other day. Gas station on the Beltway. I spotted one of them at the pump, just standing there like he knew I'd see him. I went inside, locked myself in the bathroom, and climbed out the window like a fuckin' junkie." Pilar's voice quavered, but she bit it down with a scowl. "I circled back to my car. They were gone but someone had keyed 'payback' into my passenger door."

Genevieve catalogued every detail, her mind drawing battle lines. "Damn, Pilar. Did you call the cops?"

Pilar snorted. "You think the fuckin' cops care when you're in our line of work? Besides, I don't trust them. Not after last time."

Genevieve nodded, conceding the point. "Why didn't you come straight here after?"

"I needed to lay low. Get my thoughts together. So, I rented a room in Midtown. Been watching my own back. But at this point, it's bigger than me. This ain't random, Genevieve. You know it isn't." Pilar turned to face her; eyes glassy but sharp. "What the fuck do they want?"

Genevieve rose from the sofa and crossed to the wet bar, the click of her heels the only sound in the room. She poured herself a glass of water—cold, no ice, just the way she liked it—but didn't drink. She let the condensation slip over her fingers as she studied Pilar. "They want leverage," Genevieve said finally, the words dropping like stones.

Pilar's brow furrowed. "Leverage against you? Because I'm not a boss but you are."

"Doesn't matter. You're a symbol. They know we're close. Somebody wants to use you as bait." She set the glass on the counter and crossed her arms, mirroring Pilar's earlier pose. "This isn't about you personally. It's about what you represent."

Pilar's face twisted, pain flickering across her features. "I don't represent shit. I'm just trying to survive." They stood in silence for a moment, listening to the storm clouds roll in. After a long minute, Pilar said, "So what do we do?"

"We get ahead of it," Genevieve replied. "Lay low, but not in a way that makes you a sitting duck. I'll set up a new safehouse. You'll stay there. I'll get people we can trust to monitor the perimeter. Silent, max discretion." She shot Pilar a look. "No more wandering around town like you're untouchable."

Pilar nodded. "I get it. I'm sorry to drag you into—"

Genevieve cut her off with a gesture. "I consider you family. That means something to me."

Genevieve's phone buzzed in her Birkin at the same time Pilar's vibrated simultaneously.

They looked at each other, then checked their screens. Genevieve's message was from Precious: "Need to see you. Priority One." Pilar's was a No Caller ID. She frowned, then answered, putting it on speaker.

There was only static at first, then a single male voice, disguised by a filter: "You should've left town, Pilar. Next time, you bleed."

The call clicked off. Pilar stared at the phone, then dropped it on the couch like it might bite her.

Genevieve's eyes darkened. "This is going to escalate. I need to warn Renny," Genevieve said. "If they're coming after you, then it will be me, and he'll be next."

"You're right," Pilar conceded nervously.

"I'll warn him. But first, you move tonight. I want you out of Houston until I get this under control. I won't risk a daytime transfer." Genevieve already had the plan forming—routes, cars, fallback points, burner phones. She was always better in crisis than in comfort. She put a manicured hand on Pilar's shoulder, just for a second. "We'll get through this. You know why?"

Pilar shook her head.

"Because we have a lot more to lose than they do. And that makes us dangerous."

Hours later, as dusk thickened to a viscous blue outside her high-rise, Genevieve entered her condo with the meticulous caution of a spy. She set her purse on the kitchen counter a little harder than she meant to, the sound echoing off the marble. Renny was already there, hunched over the security tablet, watching live feeds of the lobby and the parking deck with a focus that bordered on obsession.

He didn't look up as she came in. "Something happened?"

Genevieve crossed the kitchen, her heels silent on the Persian rug, and leaned over his shoulder to see the screen. "You already know the answer to that."

Renny's beard bristled as he set the tablet down, finally meeting her gaze. "Tell me. What is it?"

"Pilar. She's back. And she's being hunted." Genevieve's voice was even, controlled, but she could feel the pulse in her wrist hammering away.

Renny's jaw flexed. "You think it's Maverick?"

Genevieve considered. "Maybe. But this feels local. Personal. Like someone's got a point to prove."

Renny looked down, fiddled with the stylus. "Do you want me to bring her in? Set up the safe-house?"

"I'm already moving her out of Houston tonight."

Renny nodded. Genevieve could see the unease in him, the way his foot tapped under the counter, the half-second delay before he spoke. "I'm guessing you don't think this is random?"

Genevieve stared through the window, city lights pierced the night, their glow cutting through what remained of the storm's darkness, now a velvet blackness. "No. It's not. Just like it wasn't random last time."

Renny's silence was heavier than most people's anger.

Genevieve crossed her arms, the gold bangles on her wrist clinking softly against each other. "Look, I came here to give you a heads-up, but your face tells me you've already connected these dots. So, when are you gonna stop acting like these attacks on Pilar are a coincidence because I'm not buying it."

He sighed, rubbed his eyes. "Genesis came to see me a few weeks ago. Told me Maverick's war is still active. That it's spreading."

Genevieve's hand went rigid on the kitchen counter, her perfectly manicured nails pressing half-moons into the pale marble. The room shrank around her, all that curated elegance suddenly suffocating. "You knew and you didn't tell me?" the words came out low, full of a venom she rarely let slip.

Renny kept his cool. He'd been on the receiving end of her temper before, but this was different. This was the kind of anger that came from being blindsided, from realizing how badly you'd underestimated your own position on the chessboard. "Genevieve, listen. Maverick's been dormant for months. I figured you were finally safe for once. I didn't want to drag you back into blood and paranoia unless it was necessary."

"That's not your call!" she snapped, voice rising in the echoing space. "You think I'm some fragile princess? I would have had Pilar under protection and out of town if you'd told me."

He stared at her, then shook his head. "There's no guarantee she would've left. You know Pilar. She's stubborn as hell."

Genevieve paced the length of the kitchen, "You think Maverick sent those goons for Pilar?"

"Maybe or it could be Riot Mercer. He's a rabid dog. His brother Cortez kept him on a leash, but now that Maverick's running the show, every reject with a grudge is crawling out from under a rock. Riot's not smart enough for a full-scale kidnapping, but he's reckless. And that makes him dangerous."

She went still, letting the dread settle over her shoulders like a winter coat. She pictured Pilar crouched in that gas station bathroom, hands shaking as she eavesdropped through a vent for footsteps. She remembered how many times she herself had been boxed in, cornered, hunted like an animal. The old fear was back, but so was a familiar taste—adrenaline, and the need to control the narrative.

"I want eyes on Pilar twenty-four seven," she said. "Not just a lookout. Armed, vetted, and loyal. No freelancers. No one with a record in Harris County. You understand?"

"Already done," Renny said, easier now. He slid a tablet across the counter. On the display, four faces rotated in a digital carousel. "These are mine. I trust them with my life. And yours."

Genevieve didn't sit, didn't relax. "Good. Double the coverage. She'll make her own plans, but if anyone gets within fifty feet, I want to know before they even step off the curb."

Renny's eyes glanced up to hers—full of worry, yes, but also respect. "We'll keep her safe.

And I'll keep you in the loop from here on out. I promise."

She let herself soften, just a fraction. Genevieve's gaze drifted to the skyline, where a bolt of lightning spiderwebbed through the clouds. "If they're really coming, they'll hit us everywhere we're vulnerable. Old friends, old habits, old addresses."

Renny's hand found hers, their fingers interlacing on the cold stone. "We'll prepare. We always do."

Lightning lit the sky again, and for a moment Genevieve saw their reflections in the window—two survivors, backs pressed together, knives drawn, waiting for the next strike.

After a long silence, Genevieve pulled her hand back, grabbed her phone, and started texting. "I need to speak to Precious tonight. And keep your line open—I want real-time updates on Pilar's movement. If Riot or Maverick tries again, I want to be the first to know."

Renny nodded, already shouldering his jacket. "I'll make calls. Nothing gets past us this time."

Genevieve watched him go, his broad shoulders tense under the blazer, then exhaled slowly. The city seemed to breathe with her, the storm outside echoing the one inside her chest.

She stared at the muted tablet screen, memorized the faces of the men tasked with Pilar's life, then typed a message of her own. If Maverick wanted a war, he'd get one. But this time, she wouldn't be caught off guard.

With the first rumble of thunder shaking the windows, Genevieve felt the old part of herself—cunning, ruthless, unbreakable—snap back into place.

Justina moved through the condo with the practiced grace of someone who'd spent years curating every detail of her presence. The silk robe—oyster gray, monogrammed—clung to her hips as she drifted into the kitchen. Marcus was already there, unloading brown paper bags onto the broad marble island like he belonged in the space. He'd shucked his suit jacket, rolled up his sleeves, and was plating takeout with a confidence that bordered on presumptuous.

She watched him for a second, eyeing the lean muscle in his forearms, the no-nonsense way he handled the containers. He must've caught her staring, because he flashed that smile—the one that kept her off balance, even now. "Hope you like Jamaican," he said, the grin crooking wider. "Couldn't decide, so I got a little bit of everything from that spot on 163rd. The one with the line out the door."

"Let it never be said you don't know how to make an entrance," she replied, arching a brow. She moved closer, peering into the containers: oxtails, pepper shrimp, peas and rice, festival bread. The aromas—clove, scotch bonnet, coconut—made her mouth water despite herself.

He handed her a plate, all generosity. "You like it spicy?"

She took the plate, careful not to let their fingers brush. "Try me. I've been through worse than pepper sauce." She meant it as a joke, but the look he gave her was heavy with implication.

They ate at the counter, side by side, elbows almost touching. Conversation was easy. Marcus talked about his "nonprofit work"—mentoring teens in Overtown, organizing food drives, trying to "keep the next generation from falling into the traps he barely escaped himself." She knew enough about Miami's underbelly to guess that Marcus walked the tightrope between the street and legitimacy, but she liked the way he made it sound noble. She liked, even more, that he didn't pressure her to overshare in return.

Justina's laughter surprised her—a real laugh, not the polite smile she'd perfected since Amir's death. Marcus's stories cut through the fog of her grief like sunlight. Something in his irreverence reminded her of those younger years when she, Amir, and Aaliyah had run wild together. The memory should have stung, but instead it warmed her. For a moment, she wasn't Amir's widow—she was just herself again.

As if conjured by the thought, her phone buzzed against the counter. She ignored it, savoring her last bite of festival.

"Something on your mind?" Marcus asked, head cocked. The question sounded casual, but his eyes flicked to the phone.

She shrugged. "Just noise. Some people think I owe them my grief." She regretted the words as soon as she said them, but Marcus only nodded, not pressing.

He picked up his own phone, glanced at it, put it face-down on the counter. "You ever get tired of being watched, Justina?" his tone was half-joke, half-dare.

She wasn't sure which version of herself to answer with. "Only when it's by people who think they have a right." She let the sentence dangle.

He smiled, but the mood had shifted—more honest, less banter.

They sat in comfortable silence. Marcus poured them both glasses of wine and turned on soft music, letting the conversation drift away on the sound of muted reggae and city rain. He didn't try to touch her or linger too long on any personal question. The restraint was refreshing. Still, under it all, she felt the current—something dangerous humming in the space between their words.

It wasn't until she was clearing plates that the knock came—a sharp, impatient rattle at the door. She stiffened, exchanged a glance with Marcus. She set the plate down, brushed her robe smooth, and walked to the door. The peep-hole showed Desmond: She opened it to find him standing there, jaw tight, eyes sweeping past her shoulder. Justina's heart raced as she watched Desmond's expression darken, his presence filling the room like a storm cloud. She could feel the weight of his disapproval, heavy and unmistakable as storm pressure before lightning strikes.

He walked in with a sense of possession, his eyes lingering on Marcus. "Didn't know you had company."

Justina blinked. "Desmond, he's a friend. I mentioned to you we met at my yoga class. We just finished eating."

"Friend, huh?" he remarked, a hint of irritation.

Marcus stood in the doorway, calm as ever. "Everything straight?" he inquired, his tone friendly but carrying an undertone of confidence. He smiled easily, extending a hand. "Marcus. Justina's told me a lot about you."

Desmond didn't take it. "I bet she hasn't told you enough." He assessed Marcus with a sharpness that made Justina's pulse quicken. The air between the two men was charged, a silent challenge hanging in the space.

Justina stepped between them before the testosterone could really spike. "Marcus was just leaving," she said, her voice gentle but firm. "Thank you for dinner, it was nice to talk to someone who understands community work."

Marcus reached for his jacket. "Likewise, Justina. We'll finish our conversation later." He gave Desmond a nod—more challenge than greeting. "Maybe next time you'll join us."

Once the door shut behind him, Desmond looked at her. Justina felt the tension snap like a rubber band.

"You really letting strangers eat dinner in your house now?"

"He's not a stranger. I told you he's in my yoga class. And I'm really interested in his non-profit for empowering single mothers," Justina stressed.

Desmond turned to her, fists in his coat pockets. But you're not single," he countered.

"Amir is dead. So, technically I'm a widow, which also means I am now a single mother, as I no longer have a husband," she snapped.

Justina felt the tension between her and Desmond escalate with every word exchanged. The air in the condo grew heavy with unspoken accusations and unresolved emotions. She watched as Desmond moved closer, his presence looming over her like a storm ready to break.

"You have me. And I'm not gonna sit back while some smooth-talking clown runs game on you. I thought you were smarter than that," Desmond's voice was edged with possessiveness, his eyes piercing into hers.

Her spine stiffened, a defiant glint in her eyes. She squared her shoulders, a cold smile playing at her lips. "Judge me? That's rich." Her voice dipped low, each word like ice. "I wouldn't be standing here alone if you hadn't crawled into bed with Dominique. Remember? I built a life with Amir so Desi could have what you stole from us—a real family. Now he's gone, and here I am, picking up pieces of a life that keeps shattering in my hands."

Desmond's gaze bore into Justina, his expression a storm of conflicting emotions. The weight of his past mistakes hung heavily between them, palpable in the charged silence that enveloped the room. Justina could feel the turmoil within him, the regret and longing mixing together like a volatile cocktail. He knew he had caused her pain, hurt that ran deeper than he ever imagined.

"I... I messed up, Justina," Desmond's voice was thick with emotion, each word weighted with remorse. "I hurt you, I know that. And I'm sorry. God, I'm so sorry." His shoulders slumped, his eyes reflecting the pain of his confession.

Justina felt a surge of conflicting emotions wash over her—anger, hurt, but also a flicker of hope buried deep within. She struggled to maintain her composure, the memories of their tumultuous past colliding with the raw vulnerability in Desmond's voice.

"I regret everything that happened with Dominique. Yes, we share a daughter together.

But that doesn't mean we can't work through this and be a family. Because that's what I want. I want you to be my wife again."

Desmond took a step closer, his hand reaching out tentatively, as if seeking forgiveness in the touch. Justina's heart clenched at Desmond's words, conflicting emotions swirling within her. Part of her still loved him, yearning for the family they once were. But her feelings were complicated, tainted by the betrayal and hurt she had endured. Her heart still belonged to Desmond, but Justina feared love alone couldn't bridge what had been broken between them.

Shiffon was curled on the couch, flipping between cable channels like the noise could drown out her panic. Her belly had gotten heavier, rounder. The days blurred. No matter how quickly she thumbed the remote, nothing drowned out the high, whiney panic that knifed through her thoughts. Each time she passed her reflection in the dark window, her heart jolted—her belly was so much bigger now, hard and taut and unfamiliar, as if someone had replaced her from the ribs down.

Her ankles had taken to swelling by early afternoon and throbbed mercilessly into the night; she'd begun timing their inflation, a pointless ritual that gave at least the illusion of control. Days lost meaning. She'd wake to the acidic taste of bile, shuffle through the same three pairs of maternity sweats, and kill hours rereading the same tabloid sites until her vision blurred. Sometimes, when she slept, she dreamed of home, or Maverick's hand at the small of her back. Other times, she dreamed of blood.

The row house was built like a maze, all strange half-walls and claustrophobic corners, but the kitchen was the only room that ever felt alive. That's where Mia stood now, a human island in a sea of cracked linoleum tiles, gnawing her thumbnail to the quick as she stared out the window at nothing.

Shiffon broke first. "I'm not asking you to go against Caleb," she said, fingers worrying the pillowed seam of the couch. "I just need to know why. Why am I locked away like some damn secret?"

She meant for her voice to come out cold—maybe even venomous—but all she heard was the babyish tremor, weak and pathetic. Shiffon hated herself for it.

Mia finally exhaled, the sound ragged, and

padded over to the folding chair wedged against the kitchen table. She perched at the very edge, hands clamped so tight the knuckles whitened. "Because you are one," she said, words flat and heavy with resignation.

Shiffon's eyes narrowed, suspicion and fear warring behind her lashes. "What the fuck does that mean, Mia?"

Mia's gaze slid away. She picked at a stain on her jeans, the silence stretching again, until the only sound was the soft gurgle of the coffeemaker. When she spoke, the words came out in a rush, as if she'd rehearsed them a thousand times but only now dared to say them aloud.

"Genesis thinks you're dead. And that's how Caleb wanted it. Because Genesis told him to kill you—for revenge."

The room went weightless, as if all the air had been yanked through an invisible vent. Shiffon's mind snagged on the words, tried to make sense of them, failed, hit rewind, and played them again. "He... what?"

The syllables caught in her throat, thick and unfamiliar. Mia looked up; face pained. "Genesis ordered the hit, Shiffon. After Amir, he needed someone to bleed for it. You were the easiest target—especially with the baby."

Shiffon's skin prickled, a feverish chill running bone deep. "Because of Amir?" it sounded childish, pleading, but she couldn't help herself.

Mia nodded. "Genesis knows Maverick is the father. Makes you a liability. A threat." She licked her lips, glancing at the closed door as if even now someone might be listening. "Caleb couldn't do it. He's not built that way. So, he lied. Told Genesis it was done and then tucked you away here. Like a witness. Or a—"

"Hostage," Shiffon finished, the word sour in her mouth. Her vision blurred again, but this time it wasn't from screens. "So, I'm just... waiting to be found?"

For once, Mia didn't try to soothe her. "It's safer this way," she managed, but even she sounded unconvinced.

Shiffon pressed her palms to her face, trying to slow her breathing as her brain tripped through every memory of Caleb's tense, clipped visits, the way he always kept the shades drawn and never let her answer the phone. She'd mistaken it for protectiveness, or maybe guilt. Now she saw it for what it was: fear. Not just for her, but for all of them.

Suddenly, the front door banged open, hard enough to rattle the glass in the cabinets. Shiffon's heart seized. Mia stood up so fast her chair toppled.

Caleb's voice cut through from the entryway, loud and urgent. "We got a problem."

He strode into the living room, dark circles branding his eyes, the veins in his neck tight as cable wires. He stopped short when he saw the tear tracks on Shiffon's cheeks, the raw edge in her posture. "You told her?" he asked Mia, accusation slithering through his tone.

Mia lifted her chin, defiant. "She deserved to know. She's not your prisoner."

Caleb winced, dropping his gaze to the battered floorboards. "I did what I had to. Genesis would've made a show of it—he'd have wanted proof. I bought us time."

Shiffon wiped her eyes with the heel of her palm. "Time for what, exactly? Sooner or later, he's gonna find out."

Caleb dropped onto the ottoman opposite her, elbows on knees, hands balled together like a plea. "That's why we need a plan. And we need it tonight."

Mia shot him a look. "What happened?"

He raked his fingers through his hair, tension radiating off him. "Genesis is restless. He's got people sniffing around up here—first it's phone calls, then it's some kid shadowing the bodega. It won't take long before he puts it together." He looked up at Shiffon, voice gentler now. "I can move you again, but it won't last. This is on borrowed time."

Shiffon felt the baby kick, a hard insistent jab that made her nearly double over. She'd spent months pretending the future wasn't stalking her, and now it was here, waiting in the foyer with muddy boots. "So, what are my options? Fake my own death again? Run until I'm too pregnant to walk and just hope I can outrun a bullet?"

Caleb shook his head, gaze hollow. "I have money stashed away. I could send you out the country. You can start a new life. Genesis might even let it go if you disappear for good. But it's a long shot, and we'd need to move fast."

Shiffon's face went pale. "You want me to fuckin' forget my life here and move to another country to have my baby?"

"Would you rather stay here and die." Caleb shot back.

Shiffon looked at both of them, her voice shaky but threaded with anger. "So that's it? My life's a fucking raffle?"

Caleb flinched, but didn't argue.

A long silence settled over the room, punctuated only by the rhythmic thump of the baby against her ribs. Finally, Shiffon turned toward Caleb, voice flat. "I just want to stay alive and have my baby. If that comes down to me going somewhere warm, and no one knows my real name, then so be it."

Caleb slumped; all bravado gone. "Look, I don't have all the details worked out yet. But I swear I won't let anything happen to you or the baby." The words sounded desperate, sincere, like a drowning man swearing he could teach himself to swim.

Mia stood. "Then we need to come up with one. Before Genesis finds out the truth."

He looked at them both—two women, one swollen with new life and the other hollowed by too much living—caught in a war neither had signed up for.

"All right," Caleb said, voice hoarse. "Then we do this together."

Chapter Twelve

The Mercer Effect (Part II)

Precious sat at the marble counter in her kitchen, early sunlight bleeding through the windows. Her coffee had gone cold a half hour ago, but she hadn't noticed; she just stared through the steam left trapped inside the mug, phone in hand, scrolling through a message that made her stomach twist.

The text came from an unfamiliar number. No name. No emoji. No typo. Just five words that hit like a gunshot.

The messages were still there, stacked one after another. The first line glared up at her: ***We have Amir. He's alive.***

The number was untraceable, at least by a quick Google search. Each word hit like a hammer, precise and final. If it was a joke, it was the kind of joke that ended with someone dead.

She blinked, lips dry, rereading it until the letter started to blur.

We have Amir.
He's alive.

At first, she'd nearly tossed the phone—her nerves firing off an urgent, animal panic—but then the next message came through: ***$2 million. 48 hours. Wire only.***

You go to Genesis, he dies.

Her hand trembled. The threat landed with a physical weight, as if someone had pressed a gun to her chest and left it there, cold and heavy, refusing to move. She'd seen threats before—hell, she'd crafted a few herself, back when she was a different person. But this? This was surgical. Whoever wrote it knew how to hurt, and how to keep the wound open. Her hand trembled as she set the phone flat on the counter, as if afraid it might detonate.

Then her phone lit up again.

This time, it wasn't just a text. It was a photo. No face, just a hand—Amir's hand, she thought—dark skin, a gold ring on the thumb, a plastic hospital bracelet around the wrist. In the background, a newspaper page, today's date in the corner. The message that followed was even shorter: ***Prove you can pay. Or he dies.***

Precious felt her stomach ice over. She scrolled back, searching for anything in the messages that said this was a lie. Something she could use to convince herself this was another sick urban legend like the time someone faked Genesis's daughter's kidnapping. But the devil was in the detail, and the next message gave her none to doubt.

It was three lines, separated by too much white space: ***His middle name, Jalen. Ask about the scar above the left eyebrow. You want proof, we send a finger.***

She nearly dropped the phone.

Precious remembered that scar—the one above his left eyebrow. The blood had been everywhere that day at the playground when he fell face first off the monkey bars, soaking his Spider-Man t-shirt while he tried not to cry. Aaliyah and Justina were hysterical. She'd held his small hand in the emergency room, watching the needle dip and rise through his skin as the doctor worked. Seven years old and already trying to be tough like his father.

She stared at the screen. Her vision tunneled. This wasn't possible. He was dead. But something cold slithered through her chest now—that same instinct that had kept her alive when bullets flew and promises broke. If Amir was breathing somewhere, if someone had faked his death, that changed the board entirely. A lie you could fight; the truth would tear their world apart.

She scrolled to the start again, reading each line with a forensic coldness. The pattern was clear. They had Amir, or someone who looked enough like him. They wanted money, and fast. Any sign of Genesis and Amir was dead.

The last part made her mind spiral. Why are they coming to me and not Genesis—he'd tear the city apart, start a war, and whoever was on the other end of this message knew it. She pictured Genesis, his rage legendary, the way he'd once sent three bodies to a rival crew in a single night as a warning. No, there was no way she could trust him with this yet. But she couldn't do it alone, either.

She needed more guidance. Her thumb hovered over Nico's name. She called. It barely rang twice.

"Precious?" His voice was clear, already awake, already on edge.

She glanced at the clock. 7:06 a.m. "You alone?"

A pause, then: "Yeah. What's up?" He was on speaker, she could tell by the echo—probably pacing in his home office, the one with the bulletproof glass and the backup generator.

"Something's happened," Precious whispered, as if paranoid that someone was listening to their conversation.

"What is it? Are you—"

She cut him off. "It's Amir."

Silence swallowed the call. In the background, she heard Nico exhale, a long, slow drag. "Say that again."

She immediately started reciting the first message. Then the second, and the third. She gave Nico every detail, even the parts that made no sense: the photo, the ring, the scar.

She gripped the phone tighter. "Run that number. Find out where it's coming from." Her voice dropped even lower. "And Nico—Genesis can't know. Not yet. If this is real, we need proof first. If it's someone just trying to twist the knife deeper..." She left the rest unsaid, the implication hanging between them like smoke.

"I'm trusting you with this, Nico. No one else can know." The silence stretched between them. She could almost hear him weighing loyalty against risk.

"I got you," he finally said, his voice dropping to a dangerous whisper. "Let me find out who's playing with fire."

Precious hung up and grabbed her keys. The clock had started—forty-eight hours to navigate an impossible maze. Every path led to disaster: betray Genesis, get herself killed, or let Amir die all over again—if he was even breathing somewhere. She paused at the door, hand trembling slightly on the knob. The math didn't add up, but the possibility crawled under her skin. If Amir was out there, waiting for someone to find him, she'd set fire to heaven and hell to bring him back home.

Genesis's office was a study in discipline—a fortress of glass, steel, and bare light, kept so spartan that even the couch looked like a threat. Tonight, it was silent; the type of silence that only comes before destruction. He stood by the reinforced window, staring out at the unobstructed view, higher than the sirens and gunshots, higher than even the planes on approach. The city looked back at him, indifferent. It was a vantage you earned in blood. Genesis traced the edge of his glass, watching the rain sheet down the skyline. Only then did the phone on his desk vibrate—a single, insistent buzz. The name on the screen made his pulse spike. Maverick McClay. The last time they'd spoken, it ended with three dead in the street and a funeral no one dared attend.

He answered with the precision of a bullet finding its mark. "Using your personal line today? Must be serious," Genesis remarked arrogantly, tone like gravel.

Maverick's voice slid through the speaker—smooth, sinister, calm. "You took something from me."

"You took something from me first," he said, flat as a blade. Genesis smiled coldly. He pictured the scoreboard: his losses in red, Maverick's in black.

A pause. Then: "Shiffon." The way Maverick said her name, it hit like a bullet—no extra words, no buildup. "My people haven't been able to locate her for months. Her last known location was a hospital in Philly. You had her killed, didn't you?"

The breath caught in Genesis's lungs, but he exhaled slow, keeping the mask on. "She's gone," he said, letting the silence stretch. "Her and the baby. You brought this on yourself."

He heard it through the line—a sound, small but surgical: the pop of tendon and knuckle, maybe a bone breaking, maybe just something breaking inside Maverick. "You muthafucka," Maverick growled, his tone a razor dipped in acid. "You think you can take my blood and walk away clean?"

"I think," Genesis said, voice lowering, "that if you come for mine again, I'll erase your entire bloodline."

The line went dead. Genesis stood still, staring out at the city lights. But behind his calm exterior, a ripple of unease ran through him— something he couldn't name yet.

The truth remained hidden from Genesis— Caleb had fed him a carefully crafted lie. Somewhere in the outskirts of Philly, the woman Maverick was mourning still lived. Shiffon's hands cradling the swell where Maverick's heir grew stronger each day—and the child in her belly kicked like an omen.

The phone buzzed again. This time, it was a message. No name, just a number, no caller ID. Genesis's stomach went tight. He opened it. A photo: a loading dock in Red Hook, flooding with rain, and the back of a Genesis-branded van. The driver's side door was open, and a body—face-down, arms outstretched—was visible in the headlights. His first thought was: Not tonight. His second was: They're starting the war early.

Underneath the photo: "You have one hour to return what's mine. Or I start stacking bodies like you did." He stared at the phone, jaw clenched. He didn't recognize the number, but the message had Maverick's stink all over it. He wanted to respond but held back. Never text hot. Instead, he called Supreme. "See it?" Genesis asked.

"Yeah," Supreme replied. "Already on it. Nico's mobilizing. You want me to make a statement?" Genesis thought about it. The old him would've said yes—blood for blood, now, tonight, let the city see. But the new him had learned: sometimes you let them come to you.

"No," he said. "Let's see what they do next. But keep tabs on anyone who stands out. Use the chessboard."

Supreme laughed, a short bark. "Always do."

Genesis hung up and turned back to the window. He faced the city's accusing lights piercing through the darkness, imagining the day he'd stand over Maverick's grave, only then could he truly properly grieve for Amir, without having to look over his shoulder for the next bullet coming his way.

The abandoned print factory smelled like gun oil and concrete dust. Riot Mercer stood in the middle of the floor, a cigar burning low between his fingers, watching the flames rise from what used to be one of Genesis's distribution vans. The men who'd driven it were now zip-tied in the corner—faces bloody, pride gone.

Riot's grin was diabolic with vacant eyes. "You thought y'all could hit *my* people and walk away? You thought this was Cortez's game?"

He flicked ash onto the floor, crouching in front of the man with the least fight left in him. "Tell your boss..." he said eerily, "that I ain't my brother. I don't do clean hits. I do bloodbaths."

He motioned with two fingers. One of his men, Loco, stepped forward and placed a gun in Riot's hand. Riot stood, walked behind the man, and without hesitation—fired one shot through the back of his skull.

The sound echoed through the factory, bouncing off every steel beam.

The second man screamed. The third tried to run. Loco and Grit dragged him back, forcing him to his knees. Riot looked down at the trembling survivor. "You tell Genesis Taylor that I'm coming for everything with his name on it. Every dollar. Every soldier. Every ghost he ever buried."

He bent down until his lips were next to the man's ear. "And if he wants peace, he can find it in the dirt next to his boy."

Riot walked out, the fire behind him growing, casting long orange shadows. For the first time, his smile was genuine.

"Let's make 'em bleed," he said.

The men followed him out into the night.

Chapter Thirteen

Ghost Money

Precious hadn't heard a word in days. The 48 hours had come and went. No new messages. No pings. No follow-up. Just silence. And with every passing hour, the doubt grew louder in her chest. She replayed the same sequence of events in her mind until they blurred in a single, throttling certainty: either this was the cruelest head game, or someone had Amir alive and within reach.

For the past week, the ransom text had been her entire world—her only proof Amir's body was somewhere other than a slab.

Nico had tried to trace the number—twice. Each time, the trail died on a prepaid burner. Whoever sent the text wasn't just lucky; they were trained, calculated, and never once stumbled.

The sense of helplessness, so unfamiliar to Precious and it made her furious and desperate for leverage. Then, just as she was about to chalk it up to psychological warfare, her phone buzzed. A single text.

You have 24 hours. Have the money ready. I'll send the location and instructions. Come alone or don't come at all.

Her hands went cold.

She didn't hesitate—grabbed her bag, keys, and coat, and headed straight to Nico's loft.

The city was a rain-streaked blur outside, car windows sleeking over with mist as she parked two blocks out from Nico's loft. Had to keep up the perimeter. Genesis's paranoia was contagious now, and Precious had no intention of walking into a setup.

She clicked up the elevator, hands buried in the pockets of a blazer, anxiousness setting in. By the time she reached Nico's door, she could hear classical music behind the wall. She knocked. Hard. The whole door vibrated and then went quiet. Precious heard footsteps, the chain unlocking. When Nico opened it, he looked surprised—but not shocked.

"Precious?" he said, shirtless, running a towel over his head.

She stepped forward, about to tell him the details of the latest text message—when she caught movement in her peripheral and froze.

Kyra padded out from the bedroom, bare legs and the hem of Nico's white T-shirt barely covering her hips. Her curls were wild, the halo of them puffed from sleep, skin dewy, eyes still sleepy and she looked at Precious with a glint that was too guarded to be embarrassment.

"Didn't realize we were expecting company," Kyra said, each word measured like a dose of medicine.

Precious checked herself, then nodded. "Sorry. I didn't realize I was interrupting."

Kyra shrugged. "I was just on my way out, anyway." She ducked back into Nico's bedroom, the door hanging open behind her, and Precious could hear her rifling through drawers with rapid, deliberate motions.

Nico wiped his face with the towel, eyes flicking up and down Precious like he was scanning for bullet wounds. "You want coffee?" he asked, gesturing to the French press on the stovetop.

"I'm good." She crossed her arms. "I got another text."

That woke him up. Nico set the towel aside and reached for her phone before she even offered it. "Shit. Same number?"

Kyra re-emerged, "I'll call you later," she said, tossing a look at Nico—and then turned to Precious. "Don't let him do anything reckless." She grabbed her phone off the counter and headed out.

The door closed behind her, and the loft was all quiet static and ticking wall clocks.

Nico exhaled, then got back down to business. "What's the ask?"

"They went from 2 million cash to now five million. Crypto, if possible. They want the transfer staged at a public spot. I'm guessing they'll send an address once they see me comply."

Nico grunted. "Real old-school. They want a public handoff to minimize violence. Or they want an audience for the kill shot. Either way, they'll be watching you from the minute you leave the building. Probably earlier."

"Not my first rodeo," Precious scoffed. "Supreme has a list of possible drop sites. He's running them through facial rec, traffic cams, even

drone sweeps for repeat visitors. If we can antic-
ipate the location, we set up a counter-surveil-
lance cell."

He nodded, then scanned the rest of the
message. "You think it's really Amir? They could
be stringing you along."

"I know." Precious met his gaze, steady and
lethal. "But I have to try. If there's even a one per-
cent chance, I have to be the one who's there."

Nico leaned in, wolfish and sharp-edged.
"You'd better not get yourself shot. Genesis will
have my head. I don't need those problems."

"Speaking of problems, it seems you and
Kyra are getting serious," Precious pried.

"I wouldn't call that a problem. If so, the
good kind," Nico said.

Precious raised an eyebrow. "Nico Carter are
you smitten with Nurse Kyra?" she smiled.

"Save the commentary," he said already spreading a map across the table. "We've got bigger
problems than my love life."

For the next ten minutes, they dissected the
operation like surgeons: entry points, escape
routes, backup signals, dead drops. Precious
committed every detail to memory until the riv-
erfront became a blueprint in her mind.

She glanced at her watch—the countdown

ticking in her veins. "Twenty-three hours and change," she said, voice hardening with resolve. "If Amir's breathing anywhere on this earth, I'm bringing him home. Whatever it takes."

Riot was back in Houston ready to strike once again as he couldn't stand being ignored. Each body was a love letter, each murder a paragraph in the bloody message he was writing across the city for Genesis to read. This wasn't just business—this was personal now, a promise carved into flesh that he wouldn't stop until Genesis was in the ground. He left another body in the middle of the lot—duct taped to a metal chair, throat slit, a note stapled to the chest.

Riot Mercer stood over it, chewing a toothpick, his Timberlands flecked with blood.

The note read: ***For every piece you take from us, we take a whole damn corner.***

His eyes narrowed.

The man in the chair was one of Genesis's lower-level suppliers. A soldier. Barely made it past foot traffic. Still, he was a message—because Riot understood what Genesis was doing. Playing it cool. Strategic. Surgical.

Riot didn't like that. Cool was dangerous. Cool meant control.

He turned to his crew. "From now on, anybody that even *thinks* about moving work under Genesis gets this treatment. Word for word. Block for block. Blood for blood."

One of his men asked, "You want us to hit the Queens line too?"

Riot lit a cigarette. "Nah. Not yet. Let him think he still got control out there. Let him think he's steady. Then we gut that shit all at once."

The city was about to burn.

Justina's eyes fluttered open to the same Miami sunlight, the same tangled sheets, and the same storm of questions about Desmond that consumed her thoughts each morning. The flowers placed on Amir's casket hadn't even begun to wilt, when Justina started contemplating a future with her ex while Dominique circled like a shark sensing blood.

She stepped out the shower, towel-dried her hair as she studied her reflection in the steam-clouded mirror. Her fingers traced the familiar contours of her face—this carefully crafted image she'd spent years perfecting. Applying serums and creams in the exact order she'd perfected. The morning ritual felt like strapping on a bulletproof vest, but underneath, Justina's foundation was cracking. Every certainty in her life had turned to quicksand.

The knock on the door jolted her back to reality. She clinched the silk belt of her robe tight against her waist and crossed the cool marble floor toward whoever waited on the other side. She peered through the peephole and saw Marcus, holding two iced coffees and a grinning self-assurance so casual it had to be intentional.

"Hope I'm not catching you too early," he said. He was in gym clothes, the kind that played up his shoulders and left just enough sheen on his skin to advertise discipline without vanity.

She flashed a smile, practiced but warm. "You're fine. I just got out the shower."

He stepped inside, tracking the open spaces of her condo with a deliberate slowness. "Nice view," he said, his gaze flicking from the glass wall to where her robe parted at the knee. Justina smiled, closing the door behind them.

"You always wake up this pretty?" he asked.

She rolled her eyes, but not callously. "Depends on the day. And who's asking."

The first twenty minutes they sat on the balcony, sunlight caught the edge of every glass and steel surface, and the air felt more Mediterranean than Miami—salt, blue sky, a faint undercurrent of old money. They were talking casually—books, music, travel. She felt herself relax around him. Marcus had that way of slipping past people's defenses. He listened just enough. Knew how to look at you like you were the only person on Earth.

Then came the knock.

It was hard. Forceful.

The second knock was not a knock but a fist, hard and percussive. The sound had an urgency to it. Marcus stood before she did, his body language shifting instantly from relax to alert. He turned to her with a look that both reassured and commanded: Let me.

Justina stood, heart racing.

He cracked the door—just two inches. That was all it took. The man on the other side wore black, from the battered sneakers to the hood pulled low over his brow. In his fist: a knife, wickedly short, meant for cutting not slashing. The man smashed the door and Marcus both backward, sending Justina reeling into the entryway wall.

The world shrank to violence—the wet grunt of men colliding, the scrape of shoes on polished floor, a bottle shattering somewhere. Justina's voice left her, replaced by the animal shriek of her alarm system, which Marcus must have tripped as he fell.

She watched, paralyzed, as the masked man lunged at Marcus's throat. Marcus caught the wrist, slammed it into the door frame, then twisted with a vicious snap. The knife clattered to tile. The man went low, tried to sweep Marcus's legs, but Marcus was faster—he planted his feet, grabbed the nearest object (a glass vase from the entryway table) and brought it down with all his weight.

The vase exploded against the attacker's temple. Blood, quick and arterial, splashed onto Marcus's bare forearm. The assailant howled, clutching his head, and made for the hallway. Marcus went after him, but the man had already bounced off the stairwell and vanished into the echo-chamber silence.

And then there was only Marcus, wild-eyed and panting, door ajar behind him. For a few seconds he stared into the hallway, waiting for a return. Then, just as quickly, the switch flipped back: he turned, found Justina on the floor, and knelt beside her.

"You, okay?" His voice was rough and gentle at once.

She nodded, but her lip trembled. She reached up and touched his arm, more to ground herself than to comfort him. Her fingers left blood smears on his skin.

He scanned her face, searching for something. Maybe fear, maybe gratitude, maybe the beginning of a new kind of dependency. "You're safe now. I got you," he said, and the words were both promise and prophecy.

For a moment, all the walls Justina spent forever erecting went transparent. She let herself lean into him, breathing his sweat and cologne, the two scents indistinguishable now, both edged by the metallic aura of spilled blood. He wrapped her in the safety of his arms, fingers feather-light across her shoulder blades, and she realized the last time she'd let someone hold her like this was Desmond.

The moment lingered. On another morning, in another world, she might have dismissed it—a blip, an inconvenience, a story told over drinks. But Marcus looked at her like she mattered, like he liked the way she broke and how she braced herself against the breakage. And that did something to her—unlocked a room in her chest she'd kept sealed for years.

They stayed like that until the police arrived. Marcus explained to the officers what happened, voice clipped but clear, each sentence weighed and measured. Justina gave her statement with a steadiness she didn't feel, hands clasped tight in her lap as she recounted the man's height, the color of his eyes, the size of the blade.

Afterward, the apartment felt violated. The vase shards had been swept up, but the memory lingered in the air—part fear, part adrenaline, part something else that left her skin numb.

Justina stared at the blood-spattered marble tiles. "I left my house running from Amir's ghost only to find something worse waiting for me here." Her fingers trembled against the silk of her robe. "The one sanctuary I had left just became another crime scene. I can't stay in this place another night."

Marcus knelt beside her, his voice dropping to that space between command and concern. "Your call—I don't leave until you feel safe. Either I post up here tonight, or we find somewhere else. Somewhere they can't find you."

She looked up into his eyes—dark, open, waiting—and she felt hope.

He stepped forward, wiped a streak of blood off her cheek with his thumb. "You're safe now. I got you."

Justina's breath hitched as she looked into Marcus's eyes, the warmth of his touch lingering on her cheek. The fear that had gripped her moments ago began to dissipate, replaced by a sense of security she hadn't felt in a long time. Marcus's presence was a shield, a barrier between her and the chaos that had just unfolded. She felt a strange mix of gratitude and vulnerability, a cocktail of emotions that made her heart race.

Outside, in a sedan with tinted windows, Dominique watched the police cars finally pull away from Justina's building. She smiled as her phone lit up with Marcus's text: ***Done. She's hooked.*** Her fingers drummed against the steering wheel. The knife, the timing, the "random" attack—all pieces arranged like a chessboard. Now Justina would run straight into the arms of her manufactured savior, never suspecting that her white knight answered to a different queen.

Chapter Fourteen

The Mirage

Precious gripped the wheel tighter as they turned down the desolate road, a long stretch of nothing but cracked pavement and leaning streetlamps.

The city's edge bled seamlessly into a wasteland of derelict industrial blocks, each building a mausoleum to the old commerce that had rotted out a decade before, leaving behind nothing but the stench of rust and failure. Wind howled between the empty lots, carrying a metallic tang and the faint, sickly-sweet undertone of garbage smoldering somewhere unseen.

The warehouse came into view, hunched and decrepit, its roofline buckled as if it was half-collapsed under its own shame. The windows, nothing but dark holes, had been boarded at random intervals, some with warped plywood, others with slabs of sheet metal spray-painted in looping tags that had faded to ghostly outlines. A single streetlamp stood at the corner of the lot, flickering with a nervous stutter that cast epileptic shadows up and down the pitted concrete.

Precious let the car idle beneath the lamp, eyes fixed on the building. Nico sat in the passenger seat, as silent as she'd ever seen him, but his restless fingers played over the grip of his gun, the other hand holding his phone loose in his lap. They had come in a nondescript sedan— "Blend in or die," Precious thought.

She checked the time: 1:17 a.m. The message had said to arrive between 1:15 and 1:25 or not at all. The only other car in the lot was a battered delivery van, white paint sun-peeled and flaking, back doors closed tight, and windshield dusted opaque. She scanned for movement but saw nothing, not even a glint of watchful eyes in the darkness.

"They said this is the place," Precious muttered, her voice thin with strain. She kept her gaze locked forward, as if the warehouse might vanish if she blinked.

"If this is a setup..." Nico said, letting the unfinished threat hang in the air. "We handle it," Nico finished, his tone so matter of fact it sounded like a death sentence. He unbuckled his seatbelt and checked the safety on his Glock, then nodded at her. "We don't walk in together. I'll cover the door; you keep the bag visible. If shit goes sideways—"

"I know," she snapped back, sharper than she intended. Her nerves were raw. "Just don't get cute, Nico."

He flashed her a smile, teeth white in the gloom. "You know me. Cute isn't my style."

She popped the trunk from inside. "Let's make this quick."

The air was colder outside the car, and Precious felt it immediately slip through the thin fabric of her coat, chilling her sweat-soaked back. She rounded the sedan, pausing at the trunk to retrieve the duffel—a weighty black bag with reinforced straps. Nico followed, scanning the emptiness in slow, measured arcs, every step calculated to keep her in his line of sight.

They crossed the cracked asphalt in silence, the only sound the crunch of gravel under their boots. Nico reached the warped metal door first. He hesitated, then flattened himself against the wall, using his free hand to test the handle. It didn't resist; the door swung inward with an exaggerated creak, the hinges shrieking in protest. He gave Precious a curt nod, signaling her to follow.

Inside, the warehouse was a tomb. The air tasted of mold and old engine oil. The main floor was a vast rectangle, empty except for the scattered skeletons of busted pallets and the odd heap of grimy insulation fallen from the rafters. But someone had rigged low floodlights to the support beams, their pale blue-white beams focused on a solitary chair at the center of the space.

And in that chair—slumped, bound, head canted at a grotesque angle—was a man. He wore a blood-darkened t-shirt and sweatpants, and his face was a horror of swelling and split skin, lips puffed beyond human shape. Duct tape wound around his wrists and ankles, pinning him to the chair so tight that his hands had gone a mottled purple.

Precious's breath hitched, and for a moment she couldn't move, couldn't even will herself to blink. Nico circled the perimeter, weapon drawn but pointed at the floor. His shoulders relaxed a millimeter when nothing jumped from the darkness.

They advanced as one, the space between them and the chair closing with the slow, relentless logic of a funeral processional. Precious felt herself detach, watching from somewhere outside her body as she approached the battered man. His chest rose and fell in shallow, rattling breaths. One eye had swollen shut, the other fixed on her in bleary panic.

"Oh my God," she whispered, and the bag slipped from her shoulder, landing with a dull thud. "Amir!" she screamed running towards him.

The man made a guttural sound, trying to speak through the blood and spit pooling in his mouth. It was nothing but a wet moan, but it sent a jolt through Precious's chest.

Nico leaned in, crouched beside the chair, and studied the man's face, searching for the clues violence tried to erase. "It's him," he said, voice hushed. His eyes slid over the man's frame, noting the width of his shoulders, the set of his jaw beneath the bloat. "Same build. Same skin tone..."

Precious dropped to her knees in front of

the chair. She reached for the man's face, then re-coiled as another moan bubbled from his throat. "Amir?" Her voice broke with the effort to keep it steady. "We got you. It's gonna be okay."

The man blinked sluggishly, head lolling forward, chin slick with blood. She pawed at the tape over his mouth, peeling it away as gently as she could. He wheezed, then shivered violently, the shock of air hitting his swollen lips almost enough to make him weep.

But the sound he made wasn't Amir's. Precious knew it instantly—the thickness of his accent. And then, as she fumbled with the tape around his wrists, Nico's voice cut through her shock:

"Wait," he said sharply. "His left wrist. No tattoo."

He was right. The wrist was bare, except for a scabbed-over burn. "Amir had that lion head inked on his wrist when he turned sixteen," Nico added, locking eyes with Precious.

Precious's heart bottomed out. She stag-gered back a step and let the man's hand fall. The world faded to gray, the floodlights leeching all color from the scene. She pressed her fists to her mouth and screamed silently, only her eyes be-traying the depth of the despair.

Nico stood, face hardening as he looked the decoy over. "Whoever did this went to a lot of trouble," he muttered. "They found someone with the same build. Beat him past the point of recognition. Left him in the open, knowing we'd send someone to check."

"To what end?" Precious rasped. Her voice was ragged as torn paper. "Why go this far?"

"Psychological warfare," Nico answered, lips twisting into a snarl. "They want us off-balance. They want us to report back that Amir was alive and then dead all over again, so Genesis loses his mind and makes a mistake."

Precious stared at the beaten man; her voice barely audible. "If Genesis had seen this... if we'd gotten his hopes up..." She shook her head, fingers trembling. "He wouldn't have survived losing Amir twice." She wanted to punch the floor, to break every bone in her body until she felt nothing. But she willed herself to look again at the man in the chair. His eyes, cloudy with pain, darted between them, pleading for mercy.

"What do we do with him?" she asked, barely above a whisper.

"We can't leave him here," Nico said, stripping the tape from the man's wrists with clinical efficiency. "The next crew that comes will finish the job. He's just a pawn, same as the rest of us."

Together, they eased the beaten man out of the chair. Precious slung his arm around her shoulder, ignoring the stickiness of his blood soaking through her sleeve. They moved fast, retracing their steps to the car with the urgency of people who knew help was not coming.

The man groaned but managed to stay upright. His face was a ruin, but he clung to Precious as if she was the only solid thing in the world. She felt the tremor in his body, the animal fear that radiated from every muscle.

They loaded him into the back seat, propping him against the door. Nico fished a bottle of water from the glovebox and pressed it to the man's lips, but he could only take a sip before choking. Precious couldn't shake the image of the man's swollen face, the desperate plea in his eyes. The night had been a setup, they wanted us to think Amir was alive, to dangle that hope in front of us before snatching it away. It was a cruel joke designed to shatter them, and it had worked—almost. But amidst the turmoil, a glimmer of strategy began to form in both Precious and Nico's mind.

Later that week, Genevieve stood in the middle of an empty, opulent space in the heart of downtown Houston. The glass walls glittered like diamonds beneath the recessed lighting, and the champagne-colored marble bar curved like a whisper across the floor. Her newest venture—*Citrine*—was unlike anything the city had ever seen.

The club hadn't even opened and already it had a gravity, a pulse, a reputation. Word moved quick in Houston's social arteries—the rich, the powerful, the beautifully broken, all drawn by rumor of the impossible: a venue that would outshine and outlast every glittering corpse on Washington Avenue.

Below her, the main floor, electric gold ran in veins through the custom tiles. The chandelier above the central bar was a lattice of hand-blown glass, imported from Venice at a price no one could verify but everyone would quote. The staff, even in rehearsal, moved with the terrorized precision of Broadway dancers in front of a firing squad. Genevieve watched them for a moment pivoting on her stiletto, surveying the perimeter. The security team, ex-military mostly, blended into the shadows behind the soundboard and emergency exits. The place wasn't just opulent; it was a fortress. This was intentional, a lesson learned from too many nights where fun bled into chaos and bodies hit the floor. There would be no surprises at Citrine—at least, none she hadn't orchestrated herself.

Her assistant, Sam, hovered at her side, clutching a notepad and phone like a shield. On the other end, a parade of logistics: florists, liquor distributors, a DJ who only flew private and demanded "ambient" humidity in the booth.

"Sam," Genevieve said, voice as cool and flawless as the ice melting in her glass. "Take a lap. Make sure nobody's slacking in the VIP. If they are, cut them."

Sam was gone before she finished the sentence. Genevieve let herself exhale, watched the condensation bloom on the window above the city. She checked her phone. The messages were coming in faster now: confirm Friday, can you squeeze us in, is it true about the $40,000 bottle? One caught her eye—an unlisted number, just a string of emojis, a lion and a crown. She smiled, dark and mirthless. The right people were watching.

Later, in the candle-lit gloom of a private office above the club's main floor, she met with Renny. He poured himself a Scotch. "Not bad, beautiful," he said, running his thumb along the rim of the crystal. He brushed his lips against hers, lingering just long enough to taste his wife's lipstick. "Citrine's going to put every other club in Houston to shame. Even I'm impressed."

She smirked. "Thank you, my love. But I'm sure you're not here to shower me with compliments. Talk."

"Genesis is in," Renny said. "Precious, Supreme, even Nico—they'll all be here. Maverick won't be able to help himself. Neither will Riot. They want to win the city? They gotta show up, make a scene."

"That's the plan," Genevieve replied, leaning back in the leather chair. "But it only works if they take the bait."

"They will. You've made sure of it."

Genevieve let her gaze drift out the window. The rain was easing, leaving the streets slick as black glass. "I want zero bodies inside. This isn't a clubland shooting. We do it clean, or we don't do it at all."

Renny grunted, not quite agreement but not dissent either. "What if Maverick goes for collateral?" he asked, eyes narrowing.

"Then we make sure the only collateral is him." Her tone was absolute. She remembered too well what happened when you let monsters improvise. Renny nodded, drained his glass, and left.

Genevieve stared after him. She knew how these things went. Sometimes the plan held. More often, the plan bled out halfway through and left you to improvise in the dark.

She spent the next three days tightening every bolt, memorizing every angle. The guest list was curated to create maximum tension: tech billionaires snorting lines off their own investments, washed-up athletes desperate for another shot, criminal lawyers and minor royalty and at least one disgraced senator. Aaliyah and Angel had already RSVP'd. So had Justina, with a plus one she described as "a surprise." Genevieve felt the chill of fate in that, but she let it ride.

Every night, alone, she walked the club after hours, rehearsing. She imagined where the shooters would stand, where the bodies would fall, how quickly she could get to the panic room if it all went to hell. Once, she found herself gripping the brass rail of the upstairs balcony so tight she left crescent moons in her palms.

The night before opening, she sat in the office with the lights down low. She thought of Amir, the way he'd laugh at all this, the insane lengths she was going to for a shot at revenge or redemption—hard to say which anymore. She poured two fingers of bourbon and drank it slow, waiting for something like peace to come. It didn't.

Chapter Fifteen

The Grand Opening

Dominique spent nearly an extra hour getting ready. Hair flat-ironed to glossy perfection, edges laid with precision, she wore her favorite fitted blouse—lilac, the color Desmond always said made her skin glow—and a pencil skirt that hugged every hard-won curve. She dabbed concealer under her eyes, swept glittered shadow on her lids, and doubled down on the lip gloss, a shade of pink that managed to look both innocent and seductive. The baby's hair was done up in tiny puffs, and Dominique had let her daughter hold a Ziploc full of rainbow animal crackers as a peace offering for whatever chaos might ensue.

The morning had been two hours of nerves and rehearsed dialogue: Keep it light. Don't talk about the past. Don't ask if he's seeing anyone. Act like you damn near forgot his touch, even if your body remembers every single detail. Dominique knew she was playing herself—Desmond barely even texted back unless it was about the baby—but the old magnetism was a stubborn thing, refusing to accept that her chapter in his story was over.

She bounced her daughter on one hip as she approached the double glass door, checking her reflection, then rearranged her blouse for maximum effect. She knocked twice. Desmond opened the door, fresh out the shower in a white tee and gray sweatpants. Dominique's eyes lingered. She felt her breath snag at the sight. It wasn't just the nostalgia; it was the way Desmond looked at their daughter, face unguarded, voice dropping two octaves.

"Come here, princess," he said, and the baby half-leapt out of Dominique's arms into his.

She let her hand linger a millisecond longer than necessary. "She's all yours," Dominique said, feigning breezy indifference. "She's been an angel this morning. I packed a full stash of snacks—Goldfish, fruit pouches, all that."

She followed him inside without invitation, surveying the living room, noting the meticulous order. She set the diaper bag on the counter with a thud.

"Looks nice in here," she said, peeling off her jacket slowly, letting her arms emerge one at a time. Dominique leaned against the counter, arching her back just enough to accentuate the curve. "You know, Desmond, I always said you'd make a good dad." Her voice softened, like she was slipping into an old memory. "Never thought you'd take it this serious, though."

He looked over his shoulder, smile edged with caution. "Her and Desi are my world. Always will be."

They stood in silence for a beat. The baby pointed to the kitchen table, where Desmond had set up a tea party with two plastic cups and a porcelain plate. Dominique felt a sudden, stupid ache in her chest.

She cleared her throat. "I always wanted this for us. The... family thing." She let her gaze linger, tried to telegraph the longing in case Desmond had forgotten how to read her. "I mean, just us together. It felt right."

Desmond didn't flinch. He lifted the toddler onto one hip, keeping the table between himself and Dominique.

"I'm glad we can co-parent great. For real. But that's all it is, Dominique. I need you to re-spect that."

"I hear you. But you don't wonder? Not even a little, how it would be if maybe we gave it a real shot at being in a committed relationship?"

Desmond shook his head, jaw tightening. "Nah. We were never supposed to be. But in spite of that, we were blessed with a beautiful daugh-ter. I will always have love for you because of that."

Those words stung, but Dominique ral-lied. She never let pain last long on her face; she'd taught herself to flip heartbreak into per-formance. "Well, like you said, we do co-parent great. I just thought maybe," her voice trailed off.

"Look, I didn't mean to give you the wrong idea. I'm glad we're in a good space for our daughter, but that's it. I'm seeing Justina again. We're trying to make it work."

Dominique's face cracked for a split second. "You and Justina? Are you serious?"

"Yes. We're flying to Houston this weekend. Amir's aunt is opening a new club. Genesis and everyone will be there. We are going together. Public. Official. I thought you should hear it from me." He didn't say it with malice, just finality.

Dominique's jaw tightened, but she played it off. "Right. No worries. I'm happy for you." Her voice was sugar. Her eyes were knives. She reached for her purse, looping it over her arm slow enough to make a point. She left with a tight hug for her daughter and a forced smile for Desmond.

Dominique's phone was in her hand before she hit the driveway. She didn't start the engine. Instead, she watched the front door for a long minute, making sure Desmond didn't come out. Then she scrolled to her last text thread—labeled "Riot" with a black heart emoji.

She typed:

You hear about the launch party in Houston? Everybody's gonna be there including Genesis and Justina. Thought you should know.

She hit send, then deleted the thread, just in case.

For a moment, Dominique stared at her own reflection in the rearview mirror, searching her face for regret. She found none. The city was a chess board, and she had just moved her queen.

Downtown Houston was on fire. Luxury cars curved the block like a Maybach parade. Paparazzi hovered at the edges while black-suited security kept them in check. The entrance to Citrine shimmered under a canopy of gold lights, guests stepping onto a custom marble carpet lined with white orchids and velvet ropes.

Inside, it was next level. Think Dubai meets Harlem meets Houston opulence. Crystal chandeliers, mirrored walls, plush cream-and-gold seating, and bartenders in silk vests pouring champagne like water. The VIPs were dressed like royalty.

Genevieve wore custom LaQuan Smith, emerald green with a deep plunge and sharp shoulders. Renny, in a black satin Tom Ford tux, moved like a king beside her. Precious stunned in a blush pink beaded gown; long hair swept into a bun that showed off her diamond collar. Supreme matched her clean in black on black with rose gold cufflinks. Nico wore midnight navy, crisp and lethal. His arm was around Kyra, who turned heads in a silver fringe dress that danced with every step. Aaliyah and Angel arrived draped in couture—one in white, the other in red. Both serving face and attitude.

And then came Justina and Desmond. She wore a deep chocolate satin gown with a thigh-high split and low back. Her curls cascaded down her shoulders, and her skin glowed like firelight. Desmond matched her elegance in a clean tan suit and loafers. The room whispered as they entered.

At the bar, Precious caught it all. "So, they really made it official," she said, sipping her drink.

"Mmmhmm," Kyra murmured, never one for drama but loving the tea.

In the ladies' room, all elegance vanished. Justina stood alone, pressing a fresh coat of gloss to her lips, the click of the applicator steadying her nerves. Her whole look was by design: every curl, every inch of skin, every diamond, a carefully arranged shield.

She was almost finished when she caught movement in the glass. Not a reflection, but a shadow—two, actually, bearing down on her with the precision of guided missiles. Aaliyah and Angel, their heels striking marble tile in perfect unison, entered not with the false camaraderie of party girls but the icy intent of an intervention.

Justina didn't wince. She'd worn armor her

whole life. She tucked the gloss, squared her shoulders, and only then turned to face them. "A family reunion?" she said, voice level, refusing to look away.

"I see you're still a ballsy bitch," Aaliyah began, arms crossed so tight her biceps flexed under the white silk of her dress. Her hair was pulled up, exposing a line of tattoos at her nape.

Angel stepped beside her sister, dressed head-to-toe in Valentino red, lips painted to match. Her glare was razor sharp. "Coming here like you still part of the family. Amir's barely cold, and you already parading around with Desmond?"

Justina felt the words land, blunt as a pistol whip. But she held her ground. "First of all, I will always be family. Genesis and Talisa are Desi's grandparents. Either deal with it or stay the fuck out my way. Besides, we're here to support Genevieve. I got an invite just like the two of you. That's why you're here, right? Or did you fly in just to give me shit?"

Angel was the first to break eye contact, scanning the room to make sure they were alone. "Don't flatter yourself," she scoffed. "You're not the main character. Not here. But we will call you out on your bullshit. You could've left your plus one back in Miami. None of us needed to see you draped all over Desmond like a low budget hoe."

"Sweetheart, there is nothing low budget about me," Justina smirked. "But you know what, I'm going to be the bigger person and excuse these petty and juvenile jabs. I get it, you're both grieving. But don't project on me. I loved Amir too. We grew up together, but you already know that Aaliyah," Justina said, resting her eyes on her former best friend.

Aaliyah's smile was a small, cold thing. "Did you love him? Or did you just get knocked up and marry him to spite me? You know I am the one Amir truly belonged with."

Angel moved in closer, voice dropping. "You're a placeholder, Justina. Always have been. And when that hits you again, just remember—Amir gave you grace. The rest of us? Not so much."

They brushed past her, the scent of oud and citrus trailing in their wake, heels echoing down the corridor.

Left alone, Justina gripped the edge of the sink. She met her own eyes in the mirror, seeing the mask slip for half a second: grief, shame, then something like rage. She ran cold water over her wrists, breathing deep, refusing to let anyone see her cry, not tonight, not ever.

Back on the main floor, Nico and Kyra slow

danced beneath a waterfall of LED lights. Precious and Supreme held court in the VIP with Genesis, Renny and Genevieve, who now wore a tiara of white lilies. Waiters sailed past with trays of uni shooters and gold-flecked macarons. The air shimmered with anticipation and secrets.

At ten o'clock sharp, the club lights dimmed, and a hush fell, as if an unseen hand had pressed pause on the world. In the spotlight, Genevieve appeared at the top of the staircase, every inch the CEO, her emerald gown catching the light in liquid ripples. Renny offered his arm, but she descended alone, expression solemn, holding the crowd in the palm of her hand.

Genevieve stepped onto the stage in front of the DJ booth. The crowd hushed as she took the mic.

"Tonight is more than a grand opening. It's a tribute." Her voice rang through the room. "To legacy. To resilience. And to my nephew, Amir Taylor. A young king taken too soon. One of our VIP lounges will be named in his honor. Because even in his absence, he will always have a seat at the table."

A solemn round of applause followed. Glasses raised. Eyes misted. Genesis nodded once from his corner booth, drink untouched.

Outside, a black SUV parked across the street. Riot Mercer sat in the backseat, chewing gum slow, eyes locked on the club through binoculars.

"They all in there?" he asked his man in the front.

"Everybody. Genesis, his crew. Even the girl."

Riot smiled. "Showtime," he said, lifting a burner phone and hitting send.

Inside the club, Genevieve's assistant Sam looked at his phone and paled. He rushed toward Genevieve and whispered something in her ear. Genevieve froze.

"What is it?" Renny asked, standing.

Sam turned the screen. It was a photo. A video clip.

Caption: ***Thought you'd buried him. Guess again.***

Genevieve's knees gave out.

Chapter Sixteen

When Ghosts Breathe

Genevieve stared at the image on the screen, her chest heaving. Her eyes locked on the young man in the video. Same jawline. Same eyes. Same fear. Amir. Renny caught her just before her knees hit the floor.

"Get her some air!" Precious barked, guiding them toward the back.

"No," Genevieve gasped, clenching Renny's jacket. "Don't move me. Play it again."

Sam, hands trembling, tapped the screen. The short clip played once more. No sound, just footage. Amir, tied to a chair in what looked like a basement. The video panned in slow, deliberate zoom. A fresh bruise on his temple. Lips moving—but no audio.

Genevieve touched the screen like she could pull him out. "It's him."

Precious moved beside her. "Send it to me."

Genevieve nodded. Sam air-dropped the clip to Precious, who immediately forwarded it to Nico.

Nico, who was already pulling Kyra away from the crowd. "Stay in the VIP. Don't leave until I come back," he told her, kissing her cheek before weaving through the crowd and straight into the war zone. Supreme joined him seconds later, the two men reading each other with a glance.

"Amir?" Supreme asked, stunned.

"No, this is not, Amir," Nico muttered. "It has to be Maverick. Doing his best to fuck with Genesis's head."

They reconvened in the back office of Citrine. Genesis arrived last; expression unreadable, flanked by security. Genevieve handed him the phone.

He watched the clip once. Then again. And a third time. Still, he said nothing.

Talisa's voice echoed in his memory: *"You*

think the dead stay quiet just because they're gone?"

Genesis ran a hand over his mustache. "Where was this sent from?"

"Burner," Nico said. "Same number that hit Precious about the ransom a couple weeks ago. They said they had Amir. We went and it was nothing but a decoy. They're doing it again. Someone is going through a lot of trouble to make it appear to be Amir, but it isn't him."

"So, it isn't Amir," Genevieve whispered.

Genesis didn't move. "Why am I just hearing about this. Why didn't you tell me?" he finally asked, voice hoarse.

"Because I told him not to," Precious stepped forward and said. "I didn't want you to lose Amir twice. I'm sorry, I shouldn't have brought Nico into it."

Nico sighed. "Yeah, you should've. Genesis, we can't allow Maverick, Riot or who the fuck ever is trying to break you to make us distracted. We gotta stay focused on taking those muthafuckas out."

"You right. It's time to kill something," Genesis growled.

Meanwhile in a safehouse on the outskirts of Houston Riot flicked a lighter on and off, watching the flame kiss the tip of a blunt he never actually smoked. He stood over a burner phone as his man paced behind him.

"You think they bought it?" the man asked.

Riot grinned. "They bought it. They feasting on fear right now."

"Boss ain't say to send the video though."

"I don't give a fuck what Maverick said," Riot replied, eyes locked on the screen. "They need to know we still got power. Genesis think he's untouchable. Nah. He just hasn't bled enough yet."

"But what if they trace it?"

"They won't," Riot said. "And even if they do—let 'em come."

He clicked the remote. A monitor blinked to life. There, tied to a chair, beaten but breathing—wasn't Amir. It was another kid he found who *looked* like Amir. Close enough for a video in dim light. The real Amir? Riot had no clue where he was buried. But the rumor was enough. Chaos was currency.

The next night at what could only be described as a war room, the core circle was in place. Genesis, Supreme, Nico, Precious, Renny, and Genevieve sat around a long table in a private location above a closed-down jazz bar Genesis owned under a shell company.

"The video's a fake," Nico said finally. "I've cross-referenced timestamps. It was filmed yesterday. The kid isn't Amir, but they knew what they were doing. The lighting. The bruising. The fear. It was meant to rattle us."

"And it did," Genevieve admitted.

"Good," Genesis said. "Let them think we're shook."

He pulled up a map of Houston. Red dots blinked across the screen.

"We've been tracking Riot's men. At the end of the week, we make our move in Newark. We smoke out their supply points. Strip their power. We don't just retaliate—we erase their presence."

"What about Maverick?" Genevieve asked.

Genesis's eyes went cold. "He's next."

Desmond sat on the edge of his bed, the room lay shrouded in the kind of stillness that always came late at night—the city's distant white noise seeping through the cracked window, the air thick with the mingled scent of candle wax, laundry softener, and the trace of Justina's perfume. He ran his hand across her bare shoulder, thumb feathering slow circles along the tendons, not trying to fix her, just holding her here in the present.

"You, okay?" his words came rough-edged with fatigue but steady with certainty: "Talk to me."

Justina twisted the edge of the sheet between her fingers. "When Dominique dropped off the baby earlier, I caught her looking at our family photos. The way she stared at them..." She shook her head. "I don't know. She's always had that edge, but this was different."

Desmond's jaw tightened. "She can look all she wants. I made my choice." He took Justina's hand, stilling her nervous movement. "She'll have to learn to live with that. We're a family now—you, me, and Desi. That ain't changing."

She nodded slowly, but her mind was now elsewhere. She thought about Marcus. He was everywhere and nowhere, and every time she tried to picture him as a person with a life of his own, she drew a blank.

Then the other day when she got back from Houston, she was nearly run off the road leaving the condo; Marcus had been around the corner, somehow, and had walked her back upstairs, offering to call the cops or handle it like he did before. Sometimes it seemed like Marcus was the only real thing in her world, the only thing she could count on—except, lately, that reliability was starting to feel less like safety and more like surveillance.

"I keep thinking about Marcus," Justina said out loud.

Desmond's grip tightened. "He always knows when to show up. Even before I ask. Like he's waiting for me." She sat up, the blanket slipping to her waist.

Desmond didn't answer right away. He stared at the wall, running the timeline in his own head. He'd always been suspicious of people who tried too hard to be invisible, and Marcus was the definition of a shadow.

"Maybe I'm being paranoid," Justina mumbled, biting the inside of her cheek. "It just feels like he's...watching. Like he's keeping score for someone else."

Desmond's voice dropped, flat and certain. "Nah. You ain't wrong."

She looked at him, surprised.

He met her eyes. "I don't trust him either."

Justina let out a sigh of relief, as if she'd been waiting for someone to validate the itch at the base of her skull. "What the fuck do you think he's after?"

Desmond's eyes hardened. "Don't know yet," he said, voice tight. "But I'll find out." He turned back to her. "Stay strapped. Keep that phone charged. And don't let nobody through that door that ain't me. If Marcus got his own agenda or if he's somebody's puppet, trust I'm gonna find out who's pulling those strings."

The wind outside howled through skeletal trees, but inside the dimly lit house, there was only tension and the sharp, rhythmic breathing of a woman in labor.

Shiffon gripped the edges of the sofa, sweat pouring down her temple as a contraction twisted through her body. Her cries were low, muffled by the biting of her lip. A middle-aged woman in scrubs — a trusted midwife Caleb had on retainer — moved around the room with quiet efficiency. The house smelled of antiseptic and storm-soaked wood.

"You're doing great," the midwife soothed, brushing Shiffon's damp hair back. "One more push."

Shiffon bore down with everything in her, fingers digging into the throw pillows. A scream ripped out of her throat as the pain crested, then—A high-pitched cry.

The midwife caught the baby in her arms, wrapping him swiftly in a warm towel.

"It's a boy," she said gently, offering the crying newborn to Shiffon.

Tears streaked down Shiffon's face. "My son..." she uttered, clutching him to her chest. "You're safe now. I swear it."

Behind them, Mia stood frozen in the doorway, face pale, one hand pressed to her lips. Caleb appeared moments later, breathless, his eyes wide with awe and something deeper relief, maybe. Or guilt.

"She okay?" he asked the midwife.

"She's strong," the woman replied. "And the

baby's healthy. You did good bringing her here when you did."

Shiffon looked up at him, eyes heavy but searching. "Is it time?"

Caleb gave a subtle nod. "Yeah. Everything's ready."

A week later on a back road leading to a private airstrip the rain had stopped, but the roads still glistened under the blur of streetlights. Caleb drove in silence, hands tight around the wheel, glancing over at Shiffon every few seconds. She was cradling the baby against her chest, wrapped in a navy-blue blanket. A diaper bag, a duffel filled with cash, new clothes, and a passport under the name *Savannah Brooks* sat at her feet.

Shiffon broke the silence first. "You sure about this?"

Caleb nodded without looking at her. "Your name's clean. The passport's been scanned and verified. Driver's waiting on the tarmac. They'll fly you to Lisbon first. From there, your contact will take over."

She stared out the window. "You really think Genesis won't find me?"

"I think if he does, he won't leave a newborn

baby without his mother." He paused. "But I'm not betting your life on that."

They pulled into a gravel lot at the edge of the airstrip. The small private jet waited, humming softly. A man in a windbreaker stood near the stairs, scanning the surroundings.

Caleb shifted into park, then turned to her fully. "You don't owe me anything for this."

Shiffon looked at him, eyes rimmed in red. "But I do. You saved me and my son. You lied for me."

"I protected my mistake," he said softly. "Doesn't make me noble."

There was a beat of silence between them. One soaked in history, decisions, regrets. Then she leaned across the seat and kissed his cheek.

"I'll never forget this," she said. "Neither will he."

Caleb opened the car door for her. As she stepped out, still clutching the baby, his phone buzzed. He glanced at the screen.

Unknown Number. No name. Just a message: ***Blood always finds its way home.***

His gut turned. He looked back up at the jet, then at the empty road behind them.

"Get on that plane," he said, voice tight.

Shiffon hesitated, then turned and boarded.

The engines began to whine.

Caleb stood in the rain, phone still in hand, mind spinning with possibilities. The past was catching up. And he knew—this wasn't over.

Chapter Seventeen

Final Reckoning

The air inside Genesis's safehouse vibrated with tension. Maps spread across the oak table. Ammunition clips lined up like silver dominoes. Every man in the room looked locked and lethal—Supreme cleaning his gun, Nico adjusting the scope on a rifle, Caleb silent in the corner, face unreadable.

Genesis stood at the head of the table, black hoodie over his suit, the faintest twitch in his jaw betraying how long he'd waited for this night. The screen in front of him flickered—a live feed of a warehouse compound on the outskirts of Newark.

Riot Mercer and Maverick McClay together. The final two pieces. "They won't see morning," Genesis said. No debate. Just truth.

Supreme slid him an extra clip. "We go in quiet first. Loud if we have to."

Nico smirked. "It's always *loud* when Maverick's involved."

Precious stood near the doorway, hand on her hip, phone in her grip. "I already checked the grid. Once y'all go in, I'll kill the lights from remote. You'll have a twominute window before backup generators kick."

Genesis nodded. "Two minutes is all we need." He looked around the room, eyes hard. "No loose ends. Nobody walks away."

They moved as one—black SUVs rolling out into the night like moving coffins.

Justina swung by her condo to grab essentials before heading back to Desmond's house. Outside, cicadas buzzed through humid air while cars hissed across rain-slick streets. The elevator doors parted with a soft ding, and she stepped into the parking garage, key fob dangling from one finger, stilettos echoing against the concrete. A half-formed melody escaped her lips as she pictured Desmond's plane touching down, imagined their weekend plans. Then— movement. Something peeled away from the darkness between the row of parked vehicles.

"Marcus?"

He stepped forward, smile too calm. "Didn't mean to scare you."

"You did," she said, pressing the key fob. "What are you doing here?"

He chuckled. "You forgot our talk yesterday. You said you might need help with the security system."

Her brow furrowed. "That was weeks ago. And I—"

Marcus moved closer. "You've been distracted. Happens to everyone."

Something in his tone made her stomach twist. She took a step back. "You need to go."

He sighed, slow. "See, that's the problem, Justina. You always trying to walk away right before things get interesting."

Before she could move, he grabbed her wrist. A sting snapped through her arm—sharp and chemical.

"Marcus, what the—"

Her vision tilted. The walls smeared like wet paint.

A van screeched up beside them, doors sliding open. Two men jumped out in black hoodies. She tried to scream, but her throat wouldn't work.

Marcus whispered in her ear as they lifted her. "Relax. You'll be fine. It's just business."

The last thing she saw before darkness swallowed her was the garage light flickering, her purse on the ground, and Marcus pocketing her phone.

In the Industrial District in the outskirts of Newark the night split open. Genesis's convoy cut through the fog, headlights off, engines low. They parked two blocks out. Supreme gave the hand signal. They moved fast, surgical. Dre and Midas flanked the loading bay, Nico and Caleb took the east wall.

Precious's voice came through the earpiece: "Generators down in three... two... one..." The compound fell black. Shadows moved. Boots crunched. A door burst open. The first guard went down without a sound. Then all hell broke loose.

Gunfire ripped through the silence—muzzle flashes painting the dark like strobe lights. Bullets tore through crates, sparks flying. The smell of cordite and blood thickened the air. Maverick's men poured from the upper catwalks, yelling over the chaos. Riot's voice carried through the smoke: "Welcome to the show!"

Genesis ducked behind a forklift, returning fire. "Supreme, left flank!"

Supreme rolled into position, two shots—two bodies dropped. Nico laid suppressive fire, the rhythm precise, controlled.

Caleb caught sight of Riot moving toward a side exit, dragging a duffel. "He's running!"

"Not yet he ain't," Genesis barked.

He chased him into the alley. Rain hit cold against his skin. Riot turned, firing wildly. Genesis dove, rolled, came up firing. A bullet grazed Riot's shoulder; another shattered the windshield of a nearby truck. Inside, Maverick took cover behind a stack of pallets, reloading.

"Where's Mercer?" he yelled.

"Gone!" someone screamed back before catching a bullet to the neck.

Maverick peeked over the crate—too slow.

Genesis's shot caught him square in the chest. The crime boss staggered, disbelief flickering across his face as he fell back into the shadows. Silence settled. Then another explosion—one of the vehicles outside ignited, rocking the compound. Bodies everywhere. Smoke. Fire. The stench of war.

Genesis stumbled out, not realizing he'd been shot, blood seeping from a cut above his eye, gun still hot in his hand. Supreme appeared beside him, limping but alive.

"You good?"

"Breathing," Genesis muttered. He scanned the chaos. "Where's Riot?"

No answer. Only the echo of sirens in the distance and the hiss of flames chewing through steel. He holstered his gun. "Let's move. Before the cops get brave."

They disappeared into the dark, leaving behind a battlefield of ash and ghosts.

Epilogue

Buried But Breathing...

Machines counted out Genesis's life in steady electronic pulses, the hospital room, sterile and cold. His chest barely moved beneath the crisscrossed bandages, each shallow breath triggering another green spike on the monitor. IV lines disappeared into his veins like parasites feeding on a fallen king. The fluorescent lights cast his skin sallow against the white hospital sheets, bandages hid the damage. Precious clutched her hands together near his bedside, lips moving in silent bargaining with God. Nico's silhouette cut against the window where rain streaked like tears nobody in the room would allow themselves to shed. Supreme's muscles coiled against the wall, his locked jaw the only sign he wasn't made of stone.

Supreme's voice barely carried across the room. "Doctor says he pulled through surgery."

"This round," Nico's jaw tightened. "Riot's still breathing."

Precious's eyes never left Genesis's face. She rubbed her thumb over his hand. "At least Maverick's in the ground. That threat's neutralized."

The machines filled their silence with mechanical heartbeats until the door swung open. "I need to clear the room for the night," a nurse announced.

Precious pressed her lips to Genesis's palm. "First light tomorrow, we back."

Their footsteps faded down the corridor. The door clicked shut. Minutes ticked by. The door hinges whispered, as the handle turned again. A hooded silhouette slipped inside, moving with the fluid grace of someone who'd learned to exist between heartbeats. At the bedside, gloved hands pushed back the hood.

Amir—flesh and blood where there should've been a ghost. His face had hardened into something dangerous, eyes holding the kind of fire that doesn't burn out. His hand found his father's, fingers locking.

"I should've been there," his voice a low murmur. "That changes now."

The heart monitor continued its electronic vigil. Amir leaned in, his words falling like ice into still water.

"Every muthafucka who touched you is dead. They just don't know it yet." The monitor beeped on, marking time until vengeance.

Coming Soon...

Yacht Girl

*Behind every
yacht, is a secret...*

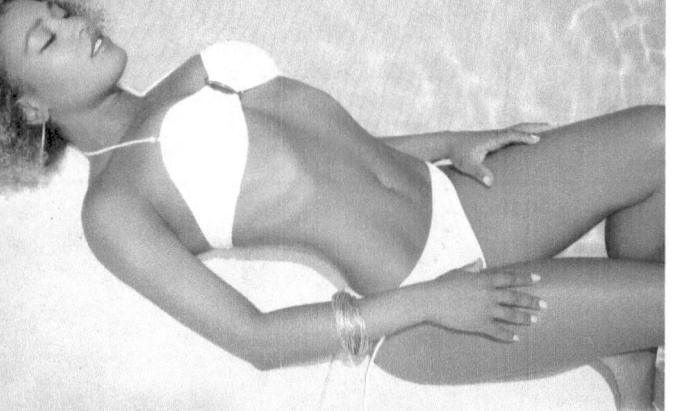

A Novelette

JOY DEJA KING

A KING PRODUCTION

Trife Life To Lavish

Part 3
Family Blood Ties

JOY DEJA KING

Pretty Lies

Chapter One

The fluorescent light above her flickered like it had a vendetta. The bathroom stall reeked of bleach and panic. Pilar sat on the toilet lid inside the women's restroom at a Greyhound station in Baton Rouge. Her heels were off. Her stockings were torn. Her hands—trembling, slick with sweat—were streaked with something that might've been blood. She couldn't even remember how it got there.

The terminal was still except for the low hum of vending machines and the occasional crackle of the intercom. Pilar clutched the burner phone in her lap like it was a life raft. One bar of signal. That was it. In her possession: a single duffel bag stuffed with scattered cash, a passport she wasn't sure was real, and a heart pounding so hard it made her ears ring. She leaned her head back against the cold tile. Sharp reality. No illusions.

"I should've never taken that first check."

Everything had started so simple. One text. One job interview. One drink. Then came the late-night calls. The apartment with the skyline view. The designer heels and private dinners. And then... the trip.

Renny O'Neal. And his wife Genevieve. Together, they were supposed to be untouchable. And for a minute, Pilar thought she could be too. But this wasn't luxury. This was a cage—wrapped in silk, disguised with champagne, lined with secrets.

"Final call for Houston departure, platform six," the intercom echoed through the restroom. Her head snapped up. That was her bus. She shoved the burner phone into her bag, yanked on her heels without buckling them, and pushed out of the stall. Her reflection in the mirror made her flinch. Mascara smudged. Eyes hollow. She looked like a woman who had seen too much and survived just enough. And she wasn't done running.

"Not yet," she whispered. "You don't break until you're out."

She paused at the edge of the hallway. Going back to Houston was the last thing she wanted. But she didn't have a choice. Not after what she'd left behind. This wasn't about Renny. Or Genevieve. This was about survival. And if she didn't finish what she started... she might never make it out alive.

Pilar sprinted toward platform six, clutching her bag. As she climbed onto the bus, she felt eyes on her—an older man in a worn denim jacket, a teenage girl chewing gum too hard—but no one looked like they recognized her. Still, she kept her head down. Just in case. Because if her enemies figured out where she was headed... it wouldn't matter what bus she caught.

The Greyhound jolted over a pothole on I-10, and Pilar woke up with a gasp. She was sweating. Her neck ached. She didn't even know what time it was. She reached for her phone—then remembered it was off. Burner only now.

In her bag was a small notebook, the one Genevieve had given her during that first "training" week. Inside were names, addresses, amou-nts. Pilar didn't know if any of it was real or just planted to test her. But she'd memorized every line. Just in case. Because deep down, she'd al-ways known this life had an expiration date. That the glamor was temporary. That the price was survival.

And now? It was time to pay.

Three Months Earlier...

The sunlight poured in through the glass-paneled doors of a second-floor master suite in the River Oaks district of Houston, Texas. The bedroom was the kind of luxury that whispered wealth, not screamed it—Egyptian cotton sheets, imported Italian marble, a walk-in closet the size of a one-bedroom apartment in Queens.

Genevieve O'Neal stood barefoot in front of a custom backlit vanity mirror; silk robe draped across her shoulders like it belonged to royalty. Her hair was styled in a soft, elegant chignon. Her nails were the color of vintage wine. Diamond studs winked at her ears. She looked expensive because she was. Not because of her husband. She'd rebuilt her life brick by brick—after every betrayal, every lie, every memory that once threatened to swallow her whole.

Now, applying her lipstick—Chanel, deep berry—Genevieve locked eyes with her reflection.

"Nichelle was a survivor," she said aloud, smoothing the corner of her mouth with slow precision. "But Genevieve? Genevieve is a brand I created."

She didn't say it for applause. It wasn't a mantra or affirmation. It was fact.

The girl from Queens who cried over Carmelo? Dead and buried.

The woman who torched Renny's favorite foreign whip after finding out he orchestrated Carmelo's death? Reborn.

Now she was Genevieve O'Neal. Wife of Renny—Renaldo O'Neal. CEO. Strategist. Curator of luxury. And most importantly, a woman who never let emotions write the terms of her life again.

Her phone chimed:

Reminder: Walk-through at The Lounge. VIP suite inspection before press preview. Noon.

Genevieve walked across the bedroom and stepped into the dressing room, sliding open the wardrobe doors. Her fingers brushed past designer labels until she landed on a soft cream two-piece set from Hanifa, paired with minimalist gold heels. The look said: refined, powerful, unforgettable. Just the way she liked it. She pulled her robe off and stepped into her new skin for the day.

By noon, Genevieve stood inside her members-only lounge, The Garden Room—Houston's most exclusive hidden jewel. From the outside, it looked like a restored art gallery: whitewashed walls, black ironwork, no signage. Inside, it was a different world—floor-to-ceiling glass, velvet booths, hand-poured terrazzo floors, ambient lighting, and music that pulsed low, just loud enough to soundtrack million-dollar whispers.

Genevieve moved through the space slowly, heels clicking soft on marble. She passed her general manager, Kourtni—a slim woman with sharp eyes—who was locking in final details for that night's wine tasting.

"Press table's set. Chef's reviewing final pairings now," Kourtni reported.

Genevieve nodded. "Good. Make sure security's tight tonight. Nobody gets past the curtain unless they're on my list."

"Of course."

Inside the VIP suite—private bar, custom art, black satin drapes—Genevieve's phone buzzed.

A text from Renny:

Heading out now. Meeting might run long. Won't make dinner. Love you. —R.

She stared at the message. *Love you.* So simple. So hollow. She knew Renny was working something behind the scenes—something criminal he thought she didn't know about. So, she said nothing. Not yet. Because silence, when wielded right, was more powerful than confrontation.

Especially when you owned the room.

P.O. Box 912
Collierville, TN 38027
❀❀❀❀❀❀❀❀❀❀❀❀❀❀

A KING PRODUCTION

www.joydejaking.com
@preciouscummingsofficial
❀❀❀❀❀❀❀❀❀❀❀❀❀❀

ORDER FORM

| Name: |
| Address: |
| City/State: |
| Zip: |

QUANTITY	TITLES	PRICE	TOTAL
	Bitch	$17.99	
	Bitch Reloaded	$17.99	
	The Bitch Is Back	$17.99	
	Queen Bitch	$17.99	
	Last Bitch Standing	$17.99	
	Superstar	$17.99	
	Ride Wit' Me	$17.99	
	Ride Wit' Me Part 2	$17.99	
	Stackin' Paper	$17.99	
	Trife Life To Lavish	$17.99	
	Trife Life To Lavish II	$17.99	
	Stackin' Paper II	$17.99	
	Rich or Famous	$17.99	
	Rich or Famous Part 2	$17.99	
	Rich or Famous Part 3	$17.99	
	Bitch A New Beginning	$17.99	
	Mafia Princess Part 1	$17.99	
	Mafia Princess Part 2	$17.99	
	Mafia Princess Part 3	$17.99	
	Mafia Princess Part 4	$17.99	
	Mafia Princess Part 5	$17.99	
	Boss Bitch	$17.99	
	Baller Bitches Vol. 1	$17.99	
	Baller Bitches Vol. 2	$17.99	
	Baller Bitches Vol. 3	$17.99	
	Bad Bitch	$17.99	
	Still The Baddest Bitch	$17.99	
	Power	$17.99	
	Power Part 2	$17.99	
	Drake	$17.99	
	Drake Part 2	$17.99	
	Female Hustler	$17.99	
	Female Hustler Part 2	$17.99	

QUANTITY	TITLES	PRICE	TOTAL
	Female Hustler Part 3	$17.99	
	Female Hustler Part 4	$17.99	
	Female Hustler Part 5	$17.99	
	Female Hustler Part 6	$17.99	
	Princess Fever "Birthday Bash"	$6.00	
	Nico Carter The Men Of The Bitch Series	$17.99	
	Bitch The Beginning Of The End	$17.99	
	Supreme...Men Of The Bitch Series	$17.99	
	Bitch The Final Chapter	$17.99	
	Stackin' Paper III	$17.99	
	Men Of The Bitch Series And The Women Who Love Them	$17.99	
	Coke Like The 80s	$17.99	
	Baller Bitches The Reunion Vol. 4	$17.99	
	Stackin' Paper IV	$17.99	
	The Legacy	$17.99	
	Lovin' Thy Enemy	$17.99	
	Stackin' Paper V	$17.99	
	The Legacy Part 2	$17.99	
	Assassins - Episode 1	$12.99	
	Assassins - Episode 2	$12.99	
	Assassins - Episode 3	$12.99	
	Bitch Chronicles	$40.00	
	So Hood So Rich	$17.99	
	Stackin' Paper VI	$17.99	
	Female Hustler Part 7	$17.99	
	Toxic...	$12.99	
	Stackin' Paper VII	$17.99	
	Sugar Babies...	$12.99	
	Deadly Divorce...	$12.99	
	The Legacy Part 3	$17.99	
	BITCH The Story of Precious Cummings	$17.99	
	Mastermind...	$12.99	
	Stackin' Paper VIII	$17.99	
	Stackin' Paper Holiday	$12.99	
	Mastermind 2...	$12.99	
	Baller Bitches Vol. 5	$17.99	
	Mastermind 3...	$12.99	
	Trife Life To Lavish III	$17.99	
	Stackin' Paper IX	$17.99	

Shipping/Handling (Via Priority Mail) $11.00 1-3 Books, $19.99 4-10 Books. For 11 or more $24.75.
Total: $_____FORMS OF ACCEPTED PAYMENTS: Certified or government issued checks and
money Orders, all mail in orders take 5-7 Business days to be delivered

www.ingramcontent.com/pod-product-compliance
Lightning Source LLC
Chambersburg PA
CBHW030331030726
47499CB00003B/731